Nicholas E

Steel

Steel

Also by Nicholas E Watkins

Tanker

Dealer

Bank

Oligarch

Hack

Nicholas E Watkins

About the Author

Nicholas Watkins lives on the Coast with his wife and has four children

He is a retired Accountant and has a Degree in Economics. He worked in

the City of London for many years.

Steel

Chapter 1

"Brass monkeys this morning," said DS Pemly. It was seven o'clock and they were driving across the flat Cambridgeshire countryside on the A10, heading towards the Science Park.

DCI Harrington was looking out of the window at the cold, January frost covered fields as the pulled off the roundabout and followed the signs to the Science Park. "We always have to either get to bed at stupid o'clock or get up at cock crow. Does no bugger ever murder someone at a reasonable hour?"

"Impressive place." said Pemly as he showed his warrant card to the gate guard at the entrance of the Park. He examined it, raised the barrier and waved them through.

"Millions invested here from all over the World apparently. It's on account of all those brainy bods at the Uni."

DS Pemly pulled the car up outside the building. "This is it "Techmat Technologies"," he said as they got out of the car. Harrington showed his ID to the uniformed policeman on the door and lifted the crime scene tape to allow Pemly to pass through. They followed the sound of voices up the stairs to the first floor.

They were greeted by a uniformed sergeant leading to a laboratory. "What's going on here?" asked Harrington as Pemly pulled out his notebook.

"Some geezer has had his brain bashed in by the look of it. Cleaners found him when they turned up at six to start their shift," came the reply.

Have you a name for the victim?" asked Pemly as Harrington passed the sergeant to survey the scene.

"Dr Stanley Huang," was the reply as he checked in his notebook. "His boss is in his office along the corridor with a PC. I though I would leave it to you lot to interview him when you are ready."

DCI Harrington was questioning the forensic team leader as Pemly walked in. They had both paused before entering, donning gloves and shoe covers to protect the integrity of the crime scene.

"I can't tell you much at the moment," Pemly caught the tail end of the exchange between the examiner and the DCI as he entered the lab.

"Cause of death?"

"It looks like he was hit over the head with the bit of equipment over there. Some sort of weigh bar or measure. I am not sure what it is used for, but it has traces of blood and hair on it. We'll test it and let you know."

Harrington looked round for anything that stood out. The lab appeared to be undisturbed, apart from the obvious body lying by the bench. "His boss, John Tatum is waiting to be interviewed in his office," said Pemly.

The forensic team, having taken photos of the corpse, were now carefully bagging it, ready to remove for the post-mortem. "Bring him here and let's see if he can spot anything missing?"

A few minutes later, Tatum appeared in the doorway with DS Pemly with the requisite bags on his feet and latex gloves on his hands. The DS allowed him to inspect the scene, closely observed by one of the forensics. "Can you see if anything has been taken, equipment, laptops?"

"Not that I can see," said a shaken Tatum.

"Ok, go back to your office, we will be along shortly," said Harrington.

"Doesn't look like a burglary gone wrong," observed Pemly. "There is no disturbance and no sign of anything being stolen."

"What can your tell us about the victim, Dr Stanley Huang," asked DCI Harrington as he sat down opposite Tatum in his office.

"He a brilliant young man, PhD from Cambridge and he was doing metallurgy research for us at Techmat. I employed him soon after the start-up."

"What exactly was he working on?"

"He was researching a stronger, lighter quality steel."

"A new discovery?"

"Not new in itself. Its composition has been known for some time. It would have wide applications if it could be produced in large quantities. It can be made in the lab but not on an industrial scale as yet."

"Can you think of anyone who would want him dead?"

"He was popular and kept himself to himself. I can't think of anyone. It makes no sense."

"I notice there are CCTV cameras all over. Can we get the recordings for last night?" asked Pemly.

"There is a central monitoring unit. You should be able to get them from there."

They drove back to the Police Station having left instructions for the CCTV footage to be gathered along with the entry log from the barrier guard. "Should be a simple one to crack once we have all the evidence back at the office," said Pemly.

"It would be nice for once, wouldn't it?" said Harrington.

Chapter 2

Charlotte laughed at her wet feet. Gilroy Jones looked up from the tourist guide he was reading as he sat on the bed. He started to laugh as he saw the puddle that had formed on the floor around her.

"There is no waste pipe."

Charlotte Carter had decided to freshen up before they took they trip into Jaipur. The basin had taps and a plug. It did not have the necessary pipe connecting the plug hole to the waste. When she had pulled, the plug the water had jetted from the basin onto her feet and legs.

They had decided to pick an old fort on the outskirts of the City in Rajasthan for their break, before continuing to Delhi where Gil had business. It had looked magnificent and luxurious on the internet. The parts that had been restored were magnificent and luxurious. The works were only about twenty percent completed however. The owner was trying to bring back to life his former ancestral home, as it had been under the Raj. He was the latest in a long line of Nawabs that had ruled from the time of the Mughals until the British had left India. He now ran a chain of restaurants in Jaipur.

"Well I didn't really like those shoes anyway," said Charlotte as she took them off and started to dry her feet.

The phone rang announcing that their taxi had arrived. The phone system, unlike the plumbing, was in full working order. "Let's move."

The Nawab had organised for them to be taken into Jaipur, where a rickshaw awaited them. The streets were chaotic and packed, the driver of their taxi struggled to get them to the point where the collection of rickshaws and their riders waited. The taxi ride itself had been an adventure. The car was, in all but name, a Morris Oxford, first made in the nineteen fifties in England. It was made in India by Hindustan Motors and renamed the Ambassador. They had stopped production in two thousand and fourteen, but the taxi owner had kept his running, just.

They were greeted enthusiastically by the rickshaw owner. He was considerably smaller in build and height than Gil and hardly came up to his chest. There were clearly some issues ahead if the terrain became hilly, the gearing of the bike could only mitigate the weight disparity to a finite extent. "Quick let us be going. The battle is about to begin," he said as they boarded and he started to peddle them in to the thong of bodies filling the streets.

Jaipur is known as the Pink City and it lived up to its name. The arch leading into the crowded old town was beautifully decorated and carved in the local pink stone. "It's beautiful," said Charlotte as they joined the queue of rickshaws to enter. There was hardly an inch of road visible beneath the feet of the thousands of people gathering for the Festival of Kites.

The festival is held every year in January and is the most colourful event in Rajasthan. The event starts at the Polo Club with a kite flying battle and spreads throughout the City. Kites of every colour and size are flown and the streets are filled with party goers for the three day event. When Charlotte realised that Gil had to go to India on business, she had checked on the internet for things to do and discovered the festival. At her instigation, they added a few days to the trip and stopped in Jaipur before completing their Journey to Delhi by train.

She and Gil had met at University and just seemed to click and were still together eleven years later. They were total social opposites. Her Father was a Chartered Accountant that had worked in the City of London his Father was a Bus Driver in Bristol. She had been to prep and public school, he to a poorly funded state school in a depressed area. She had idled her way into Guilford, he had struggled and against the odds had obtained a University Place. His parents had emigrated from the Caribbean to England looking for a better life, hers already had that life. Gil had risen all the way to the top and was now CEO of a Global steel producing empire.

Charlotte still liked the adventure in life and had opted for the partly restored Nawab's Palace as opposed to a five star hotel. Gil had enough of roughing it in a childhood of poverty but humoured Charlotte. He was four years older than her, she had been doing her BA in Psychology and he had been doing a PhD in metallurgy postgraduate when they met.

Bristol had not been welcoming to his parents when they arrived from Jamaica. They had been expecting to feel at home and in their minds eye had thought England, the Motherland, would be culturally the same as their place of birth. It was a massive shock when they encountered the reality. Cold, grey, wet and disapproved of by the majority white inhabitants, they were isolated and lonely. The work on offer was barely enough to get by on. The accommodation, if available at all to the black immigrants, was overpriced and substandard. The rack rent landlords treated their tenants like scum and harassed and hounded them from place to place, extorting as much as they could.

Gil would return from school and find his Mother waiting on the street with their possessions having been summarily evicted by a greedy landlord. St Paul's had been a hard place to grow up. Coming home from school, he would pass the prostitutes standing outside their homes on City Road. Thursdays was benefits day and they would be out in force looking for trade.

In the early days, even the trade unions had been against the "coloureds". The Transport and General workers Union had called strikes to stop black bus drivers. Gils father had born the brunt of it, but had eventually become one of the first black bus drivers in Bristol. Things had changed and Bill Morris was elected General Secretary in nineteen ninety two. The first black union leader and he did a great deal for all the workers conditions in the UK during his ten years in charge. Gil had avoided some of the early prejudice his parents had endured but it still lingered.

Money had, of course, made the difference for Gil. He had had luck, he had drive and brains and it had paid off. Now his business was worth millions and he was here in India to take it to the next level. In two days he would be meeting with the executives from Ban Dan in Delhi and he would conclude the deal of a lifetime.

Charlotte had no concept of racial prejudice. She had assumed it was a thing of the past. Her education saw her with friends of differing backgrounds and ethnicities. They stayed at each others homes, went riding together and went on holiday together. Her Father's contacts and friends were varied and ethnically diverse. She was brought up accepting people of all creeds and colours. Prejudice never entered her life. The key factor she missed was that they all had one thing in common. They were always rich.

Gils experience, coming from the other side of the tracks, was completely different. Prejudice was ever present, sometimes it had been overt, name calling or physical attack. Sometimes it had been concealed, not getting the job he was qualified for or being singled out by the police and stopped and searched.

Charlotte soon learned of prejudice when she dated Gil. Comments had been made by even those she considered her closest friends. She soon realised that the World was not the cosy place she had been brought up in. The reality, that the colour of the man she loved was reason enough for others to hate them both, was a hard pill to stomach. The prejudice had only strengthened her resolve to stand by Gil and their relationship was stronger because of it.

"It's amazing," said Charlotte as Gil come up behind her and put his arms round her. They were stood on the battlements of the Nawab's fort overlooking Jaipur. The Sun was low and the sky was shaded lilac to gold. Kites of red, yellow and all the colours of creation were flying in the sky. From small to large, from simple tri-angles to dragons and designs of all types were evident in every direction.

"It is truly an amazing sight," he responded and kissed her on her cheek, pulling her closer. "I think that you managed to come up trumps

Steel

with this place despite the plumbing, although a bit of five star luxury never goes amiss."

"We have done that. This is far more of an adventure."

"You do know we are among the first guests here? Don't you?" he said.

She looked down from the battlements onto the courtyard. The Nawab had built a fire in a brazier and the flames were rising into the night sky. Chairs had been set out and drinks were on a trolley attended by a waiter. The Nawab waved to them, beckoning them to join him to watch the Sunset. Charlotte waved back and shouted they were on their way. Turning to Gil she said, "Not only are we among the first guests here, we are the only guests here."

With the fire blazing behind them, taking the chill from the January night air, they watched the sun descend over the Pink City. "You are not drinking," observed Gil.

"I have not been drinking for some while."

"Are you suffering with an upset tummy?"

She pulled him closer. "Sometimes you can be a bit thick for such an intelligent guy."

Gil looked at her puzzled. She watched as his brain, almost like a clockwork toy, gradually got into gear. Realisation slowly dawned. "You mean you are, are, are …"

"The word is pregnant," she said.

He was ecstatic. He kissed her. He hugged her and he almost jumped with joy.

Chapter 3

The doors to the Mingyu Hotel opened automatically as Wei Feng stepped from the Rolls Royce and approached them. The doorman respectfully bowed his head in deference as he passed into the lobby. In an attempt to keep the lobby fog free, large blowers above the door sprang into action in a vain attempt to block the smog entering the building. It was not successful and it was difficult for the guests to see from one side of the vestibule to the other

The new wealth in China had caused an explosion in car and vehicle ownership. The problem was added to by the increase in demand for power as the Country industrialised. The electricity was being generated by coal, in mostly high polluting, old technologically based power stations. Emission control legislation had not kept pace and pea soup thick smog was common.

Beijing was not as bad as some of the industrial areas, but with the right atmospheric conditions, it was often impossible to see across Tiananmen Square. The conditions were right today, the Hotel Mingyu had to deal with the rapid growth in the Chinese economy and the pollution it was bringing.

Wei Feng was the head of The Changpu Corporation, roughly translated, the name meant flourishing vine. The name was aptly chosen as like a vine it had spread and grown in all directions under Wei's governance. Its core business was steel production and with State backing its factories had expanded rapidly. It was now one of the biggest producers of steel on the planet. In fact, its problem was the very fact that is was such a large producer. Following the Global economic slowdown, the demand for steel had plummeted. In order to sell their steel, Changpu were having to reduce the price. The price it was getting was less than the cost of production.

As he stepped into the lift to the Penthouse flat, Wei Feng was a worried man. The dumping of Steel was causing a backlash from other Countries, the most significant of those being the USA. The new President had made it clear that he was going to do something about it. That something would be crippling tariffs on Chinese imports into the United States.

His colleagues were already waiting, sat at the oversized table as he entered. They rose respectfully and waited for him to be seated.

"Good morning gentlemen."

There was only Meng Fan and Jin Jianjun present in the room. They waited quietly while Wei settled in.

"I have gathered you here, away from the office, to discuss the little problem that has occurred in in the last twenty four hours. I must remind you that matters discussed here remain the sole province of us three. It is not up for discussion with the rest of the board members."

Meng and Jianjun nodded their heads in agreement. Then Jianjun began to explain.

Wei listened patiently. "That does present us with a problem and one The Changpu Corporation cannot solve on its own. I am not happy about it, but it seems I have no choice than to ask for help in clearing up the mess created at Techmat."

The drive from the Hotel Mingyu should have taken ten or twelve minutes, but Wei finally arrived at the State Security Office facing Tiananmen Square an hour and a half later. He glanced across the Square and was unable to see the giant poster of Mao, just a few hundred metres away, owing to the thick smog. He presented his name to the guards and entered the building.

"Well, why are you here?" asked the uniformed head of the Service as they sat with tea being served to them.

"We need help. Things took a sudden unexpected turn and an unfortunate incident has occurred," began Wei.

"Go on," he urged. He was clearly enjoying Wei's embarrassment and discomfort and was not going to make it easy for him.

Wei continued. "There was a murder last night, English Time, and we need help in protecting the perpetrator."

There was a total look of surprise and confusion on the face of the Security Officer. "I don't understand. Why are you murdering people in England? Have you gone mad?"

"I haven't murdered anyone or asked for anyone to be murdered…"

"What, it was an accidental murder was it?"

Wei felt stupid and knew the Officer sat opposite was enjoying the humiliation. It was a rare opportunity for him to have a dig at one of the richest men in China. It was clear that this man did not agree with the new liberal approach to commerce and trade that had been introduced by the ruling Communist Party. He was at the more traditional end of the spectrum in communist doctrine.

"It has happened. We did not want it to happen. The man who committed the murder is vital to us and ultimately, therefore, to the State."

Seeing he had little choice he said, "go on."

"We have little time and it may already be too late but we need to try. They murder was at Techmat and as I said, it was not planned. Techmat is located in England on a Science Park in Cambridge. We need to destroy as much of the evidence as we can and we need to do it now."

Chapter 4

Port Talbot in Wales has the last two steel works in the UK. The Ban Dan Works sits on a site going back to the nineteen hundreds. The global glut and Chinese dumping of steel below its cost reduced production and threatens the survival of the industry.

"We need to unite and fight," shouted Reese Williams into the PA.

The assembled crowd of over three hundred men picked up the slogan and began their march through the Town.

"Unite and Fight. Unite and Fight," they shouted as they made their way to the works.

Williams smiled as he watched the mob instinct build and the men emboldened became increasing militant as they marched. He knew there would be clashes with the Police. It was what he intended. These men were fighting for their jobs and their pensions.

The Ban Dan works could not compete in the general steel market, but it was one of the few plants that specialised in high grade, hybrid steel for a niche market. That small area was profitable, but the shortfall in the worker's pension fund of around eight billion pounds made its future as a steel producer highly unlikely.

The marchers had now reached the line of riot clad police spread across the entrance road to the works. There was a little dusting of snow on the ground. White and clean, in contrast to the grim and grey of the works. Tempers were already beginning to fray. The police were not local and had been bussed in overnight to deal with the protesters.

"Break through," Williams urged. "Unite and Fight," he shouted into the megaphone.

The protestors began to pick up stones and pelt the police ranks. The police stood their ground, riot shields offering them protection. There was a standoff, calm before the storm.

Williams could not allow the demonstration to stall. He had worked hard for weeks now to organise the mob. Meetings, a whispering campaign on potential job cuts, leaflets and the internet had all played their part in rousing the work force. He needed this to escalate.

He forced his way though the mob of angry steel workers until he was at the front, facing the police line. The police were intimidating with their batons, riot shields and clad in full riot gear, their heads protected by helmets and face guards. They were trained in exactly this situation and looked formidable.

He looked left and right and saw that his comrades were hesitating and losing their impetus in the face of the well disciplined and trained police in front of them. He knew that the march would peter out unless he did something to reinvigorate the situation. He could not allow the standoff to continue. As the minutes passed the momentum was falling.

He had to act. He needed to act. He took a depth breath and calmed himself. He looked around the crowd looking for the camera crew. They were behind the police line interviewing the Officer in charge, getting his assessment of the situation. No good, he wanted them focussed on him. He wanted coverage.

"Help me and do what I do," he said to the men either side of him. He picked up a stone and threw it at the news crew. The men on either side copied his actions. Soon a barrage of stones was flying in the direction of the Officer overseeing the operation as more and more protestors followed suit.

The camera crews turned and focussed in on him as the ring leader. It was he cue. Taking a deep breath he ran forward at the policemen directly in front of him. He managed to pull down the riot shield and smash the rock he was wielding into the policeman's face. Luck was on his side. The visor on the policemen's helmet flipped back with the impact of his body against the shield and he landed his blow square in his face.

The constable staggered back, face cut and nose broken. Blood flowed profusely from the wound Williams had created. His colleague, incensed and angry, jumped to his aid and the used his baton to beat Williams repeatedly in his rage.

It was the trigger that was required. The protesters, seeing their leader being beaten to the ground, covered in blood was galvanised. They rushed the police line seeking revenge. All caution was abandoned as they transformed into a mob ruled by blood lust.

It was a pitch battle, the police charging the protestors time and time again, using their batons with maximum force. CS gas was sprayed, blinding both the mob and police alike. The injuries mounted on both sides. Ambulances were ferrying both sides' casualties to the hospital. The police vans were ferrying the protestors to the jail. The battle raged for nearly three hours.

The News that evening was full of shots of the riot. The images spread round the globe on television and the internet. The World was not aware of the problems at Ban Dan Steel. Any potential buyer or investor now could see plainly the powder keg it was and the inherent problems the business had.

Reese Williams was sat up in his hospital bed with a policeman sat beside. He was under arrest. "Turn the volume up," he said.

The policeman obliged with the remote and they watched the images of the riot on screen.

"I'm a star," smiled Williams through swollen lips.

"You're a cunt," replied the constable.

Williams knew he had done well. He would be well rewarded for the beating he had taken. They would be more than pleased with the way it had gone. The coverage was better than anyone could hope for. He had done exactly what he had been asked to do.

"Who in their right mind would want to take on the can of worms that was the Ban Dan Steelworks.?"

Chapter 5

The headquarters of MI5 was situated in Thames House in Central London. The current head of the organisation, Tim Burr, was in the daily morning briefing session on the top floor. Harry Denham, the deputy head, whose job it was to collate and filter the myriad of data gathered by MI5 held the floor. Harriet Shaw was present and specialised specifically in cyber activity, a growing area of potential espionage activity that had to be dealt with.

"GCHQ are getting very agitated and actually thinking of talking to the press directly," said Denham. The Government Communication Headquarters in based near Cheltenham and is responsible for providing Signals intelligence (SIGNET) and information to the armed forces and the Government. It listens, monitors, intercepts and decrypts any and all forms of communication. Military Intelligence established during wartime was now, in essence, left with two branches: Military Intelligence 5 and 6. The other numbered departments were merged or discontinued over time. MI5 and MI6 being part of the armed service are recipients of SIGNET.

"Well that is a turn up for the book. They are usually very camera shy," said Tim.

"It's down to the new President in the US. They have been accused of spying on him for his opponent during the run up to the election"

"Have they?" asked Harriet.

"I shouldn't think so. To be honest they wouldn't really need to. Let's face it, all they had to do was monitor the Russians. They were interfering all over the election campaign," he joked.

"Still, a bit awkward having one of your closest allies being accused of spying on you," said Tim.

"Bloody awkward, that is why they are thinking of issuing a denial."

"It's a bit like the old paradoxical question, 'When did you last beat your wife?' Isn't it? However you answer, you are dammed. If they say nothing it looks like they were spying on the President and if they deny it, it looks like a cover up."

"Moving on," said Tim. "Is there anything from them that we should concentrate on?"

"Well, there is something a bit strange and they are not sure what to make of it. I had a team look at it, but, in all honesty, they are puzzled as well. It's that strike at the Ban Dan Steelworks."

"That does sound like it has not much to do with us. Surely they are not harping back to the old days and reds under every bed?" said Harriet.

Denham shuffled some papers about until he located what he was searching for. "Emails, a few flying about that seem to be coming from a dubious source to..." He rummaged around some more, "Reese Williams."

"Who's he?" Tim asked.

"One of the ring leaders, he got himself bashed up by the old bill and plastered all over the TV news and internet. He is recovering in hospital."

"Not sure what we should make of that. Keep and eye on the situation just in case." Denham nodded.

"Anything else?" Tim continued.

"Just the thousands of cyber attacks from Russia, China and all the usual suspects, trying to infiltrate our systems, although most are targeted at big business," said Harriet.

"Is there anything specific we should be aware of?" said Tim.

"There was an attack on the CCTV system at a Cambridge based science park that was a bit odd. They wiped all the footage for a few hours."

"Do they have any industries based there that could be security sensitive?"

"Not that I can see, just the usual mix of high tech and biotech stuff. They do have one of the biggest games software writers on the Park though. "Invaders of Zeon" it is called."

"That does not sound like that would be a National Security Threat," said Tim.

"Good game though," said Harriet.

"Please stop, you are making my head hurt. I have enough work without having to consider Invaders from the planet nod."

"Zeon," said Harriet.

"Both of you stop. So the hot topics you have brought to my attention are a industrial dispute in an industry that is no longer a significant part of this Country's economy and a computer game. Is that it for today?"

"Well, there was an attempt on the electricity grid," said Harriet.

"Well that sounds more threatening," said Tim.

"Not really, there are about thirty attempts daily. This was from a thirteen year old schoolboy in Manchester."

"Very funny, now get on with some proper work," said Tim.

They left the room and Tim, back in his chair, returned to the report on the deaths of three Russian businessmen on Remembrance Sunday the previous year. There were anomalies and it was clear that the police wanted to pursue the matter further.

A bomb had been planted in their car and that bomb's construction clearly had the hallmark of ISIS all over it. The unresolved issue was, how it got in the car and how the car ended up picking up the passengers. The driver had disappeared. They wanted to track him down.

MI5 had the three Russians under surveillance in a joint CIA operation. The police wanted answers. Tim could not let them have those answers. Those answers would lead to more questions that would be very embarrassing.

Tim wrote, "Declined, overriding National Security Interest".

Chapter 6

Here boy, Seb, Seb," Matthew Watling watched as the Blenheim spaniel totally ignored him and carried on running in the wrong direction. He loved the dog and it was very affectionate, but when it came to doing dog things, like fetch or sit, it was not up to the mark. It appeared to be deaf, have no sense of smell and no sense of direction. The King Charles Spaniel had been bred as a retriever or gun dog. It was supposed to locate stuff and bring it back. Sebastian did not.

Matthew could throw a ball and Seb would return with a twig or a stone and forget all about the ball. Matthew would then have to go and look for the ball himself, which rather defeated the purpose of the dog master relationship. Seb was currently barking at a pigeon sitting in a tree. Being a King Charles, it had long ears that would constantly get in its way or fall in its food bowl when eating. It appeared that at this precise moment Seb was trying to use his ears as wings, jumping up and down in agitation at the lack of response by the bird, it looked like they were being flapped.

Matthew realised that he should have to walk over further into the wood and retrieve his dog. The woodland was only a few miles from his home on the outskirts of Cambridge. He would drive here with Seb, park up and take him for a walk most days. He had finished his night shift and having had a sleep, he would walk the dog, get himself a meal and start work at six in the evening,

He finally got Seb's attention when, as he approached the tree, the pigeon took flight. "Come on ball," he said hopefully, showing it to the dog. It did all the right doggy things, jumping up and down, crouching, barking and wagging its tail.

Encouraged, Matthew threw the ball. Seb chased off, tail wagging, however in totally the wrong direction. Matthew set off to retrieve the ball and Seb gathered a stone to bring back to his master,

Matthew had been a policeman for many years and before that had been in the army. Now, approaching retirement age, he had a job as a security guard. The hours were inconvenient, the night shift. He did not mind the anti social hours though. He had been married twice, but neither of his ex wives kept in touch. Being a soldier and then a policeman did not make for a stable home life. Both wives had become fed up with the long periods of being on their own and found alternatives. He couldn't really blame them.

He now he lived alone with his dog that seemed quite happy with a restricted social life, only having an interest in sleeping, eating and not retrieving a ball thrown for it.

He looked at his watch and realised he needed to get a move on. He became aware that Seb seemed to have disappeared into the undergrowth and not put in an appearance for some while. Sighing, he made his way to the spot where he had last seen the dog enter into the denser vegetation of the trodden path.

The park was not busy, but there were one or two people walking or walking their dogs. Most were having far more success than he in actually remaining in contact with their pet. He did wonder if perhaps dog training classes were called for as he peered into the undergrowth calling his dog's name.

There was no response. Distracted by another bird, insect or even a leaf. He assumed that Seb had forgotten the reason they were at this location was for walking. There was still no sound as Matthew made his way further off the pathway in to the woods. He was becoming quite irritated with the dog's lack of response as he wandered in the woods.

He stood still and listened to see if he could hear any sound of disturbance in the thick, ground covering foliage. The ground between the trees was mostly covered with thick patches of ferns, being the time of year it was. He thought he heard something to his right and walked towards it.

As he entered the small but dark clearing in the trees he could see Seb crouching in the centre, almost surrounded by bracken and ferns. "Seb, Seb," he shouted loudly,with annoyance in his voice. The dog did not respond, "for fucks sake," he said as he was forced to walk over to the animal.

The dog was unmoving. Matthew knelt beside Seb confused. Then he saw the red puddle spread around the still body. He reached down to stroke his pets head. As he did so it flopped to one side. The head had almost been completely severed from the body. Matthew leapt up, shocked and nauseous he staggered back from the corpse.

He died hardly realising he had been attacked. The attack had come silently from behind and the Sharp knife had sliced effortlessly through the skin, tissue and sinew of his neck. He gurgled as the blood entered his airway and flooded his lungs. He lowered next to Seb as he died, drowning in his own blood.

****

"What the fuck is going on?" said DCI Harrington as they drove to the woods, "There are bloody murders all over the shop."

"In here, I think," said Pemly as he pulled off the road into the parking area. He pulled up behind the array of police vehicles, ambulances and crime scene vans. He noted that there was a distraught woman and her dog being comforted by a WPC towards the corner of the parking area.

The WPC, seeing Harrington and Pemly get out of the car, came across and addressed them "She was walking her dog and it disappeared off into the woods. She followed it in and found it sniffing the deceased."

"OK, take her statement and we will follow up on it later," said Harrington.

They made their way to the crime scene. "What have we here?"

"Male in his late fifties, early sixties, throat cut and a dog, also with its throat cut."

"ID?" asked Pemly.

"Not at the moment," replied the sergeant.

Harrington approached the Scene of Crime office and together they looked down at the body of Matthew Watling. "He was recently killed, no more than an hour. The blood is still warm and viscous," he said.

"Anything else you can tell me at this stage?"

"Whoever did it knew what they we doing. I really would not like to meet him, that's for sure."

Chapter 7

"You have to be Joking?" said Gil as they settled into their seats on the train to Delhi. The carriage was packed with the sights, sounds and smell of India. They had reserved seats and had the help of the porter to get to them. It had been chaotic getting themselves installed in their seats, but they had avoided most of the mayhem taking place around them.

"I told you that I wanted the full Indian experience," teased Charlotte.

Gil was not that happy with his full Indian experience. "We could have flown, plane helicopter, luxury limo, instead, we are crammed in like sardines."

"Stop being a grouch. This is fun." Gil's face looked like he was a long way from having fun.

Matters were not being helped by the fact that their fellow passengers were unashamedly staring at them. The locals had obviously not been taught by their parents that it was rude to stare. Admittedly, a six foot four black man and a five foot eight redhead was an unusual sight on the morning train, but the ogling was beginning to irritate Gil. If he left Charlotte unattended, for even a few moments, a group of men would gather around her and just stare, She had not helped her cause by wearing a lightweight summer dress that was just a bit too revealing, by Indian standards, of her cleavage.

"Do your wives not have tits?" Charlotte had shouted at the group of eight or so men that had surrounded as they had waited to board the train. The outburst had no effect on the group of men, they continued to stand and stare, but the commotion attracted the attention of

28

another three or four who joined the boob watch. With the help of the porter, Gil had pushed their way through Charlotte's fan club and made their way to their seats.

A small boy was walking along the isle between the sets selling bottles of water. Charlotte felt sorrow and urged Gil to buy. He overpaid for the water and passed it to Charlotte. She unscrewed the top and raised the bottle to her lips.

The elderly Indian gentleman sitting opposite leant forward and spoke." I should not drink that if I were you."

"What," said Charlotte, slightly surprised at the intervention.

"I do not recommend that you drink the water," he repeated.

Charlotte pulled the bottle from her mouth and examined it. It looked fine. She glanced quizzically at the man.

"The boys are orphans, they are not employed by the railway. They sleep on or near the stations and make a living anyway they can. Some recycle plastic or metal. Others help with the passengers' bags and others are helping the dabbawalas."

"My name is Chadu Nathwana," he offered Gil and Charlotte his hand. Names and handshakes exchanged he continued. "The trick is that the water is not bottled water but from any source available. I fear that you will become quite unwell should you drink it."

Charlotte looked at the bottle. "The seal seemed in tact," she said.

"Ah, yes the poor of India are very resourceful. They have to be to get by. Everything is recycled and put to use if it can be. Everything can be fixed or repaired by someone from tyres to engines, taps to baths anything and everything, "

"They find old bottles, fill them with water and reconstruct the tops and sell them to tourists?" said Gil.

"Exactly, so I say it is best to not be drinking it. We prefer to eat and

29

drink food prepared by our wives rather than strangers."

"That cannot always be that convenient," said Charlotte.

"Oh but it is. As I said, we are very resourceful. In Delhi, for example, there is an army of dabbawalas that deliver thousands of hot meals from home to the desks of the office workers. The same is true in Mumbai and most of the major cities. The husband will go off to work and later his wife will prepare a delicious home cooked meal and pack it in his lunch box. The dabbawalas will collect the box, cycle or walk and take it to central point. From there, to the train station from where they will take it in to the centre of the city. The process is then operated in reverse. Thousands of boxes are sorted into routes and then delivered to the worker at his office in time for lunch."

"Why not just get food delivered from a local shop?" asked Gil.

"Cost is part of it," said Chandu, "but we are also a very diverse population in our customs and beliefs. We have many different dietary requirements."

"India is truly an amazing place," said Charlotte.

"I have always thought so to," nodded Chandu.

The journey time flew by. The countryside was fascinating and there was always something happening as the came into or left a station. Charlotte squeezed Gil's arm each time she observed something new.

The train finally arrived in Delhi. "Oh my God," said Charlotte as the joined the thong of humanity to exit the station. There were people everywhere, a sea of moving bodies. It seemed like total chaos but somehow it functioned.

They eventfully arrived outside the station and Charlotte approached one of the many cabbies vying for their business. "Hold on," said Gil. He put his hand on Charlottes' arm. "I think you'll find that we already have a taxi booked."

"Mr Jones, The Leela Palace welcomes you," said the chauffer as he opened the door to the Rolls Royce phantom. "I am at you disposal for the length of your stay."

Charlotte was far from happy, "You know I didn't want this. I have booked us into a traditional Indian Home while we are here. We were to have a genuine experience, be part of daily life. Not the five stars you could be in any hotel anywhere in the World, cocooned from reality."

"I know, but I promise it is only for one night. We will check into both your hovel and my Palace and tomorrow, after I have had my business meeting, we will move. I have to make the right impression. One night, I promise and you can take charge again."

Charlotte was placated. "It is a nice car, perhaps we should get one," she smiled as they drove into New Delhi.

Chapter 8

"Well, we need to do something. That much is obvious at least," said Tim. He and Denham were sat around the coffee table in Denham's office.

"It was not a fun meeting. I honestly did not have a clue what they were talking about. I mean, when did someone's bloody pension fund become our concern?"

"Well, I suppose it comes under the heading of industrial sabotage," hazarded Tim, hopefully.

"What! A bloody strike in steel works, in an industry that hasn't been competitive in donkey's years? It doesn't need sabotaging, it is quite capable of doing that all by itself."

Tim laughed. "So why is the Department for Business, Energy and Industrial Strategy suddenly so interested? What do they make there that is so important?"

"Steel," replied Denham.

"You are a funny man. Did you know that?"

"Well what do you think they make at a steel works? To be honest it has nothing to do with what they make, it is all to do with this idea of Brexit. Britain first, we can do it, all that sort of stuff. It looks bad if the first thing that happens post Brexit, is that the last remaining Steel production facility in Wales closes."

"Ok, so based on that, the Department has decided that we are under attack, under attack from whom? In fact, does anyone, apart from the workers and the Department of Business, Energy and whatnot, give a fuck?"

"We do now," said Denham.

"Apparently so, send someone down to check it out."

"Couldn't the police send someone undercover? We don't have much in the way of spare resources."

"Did the Department ask the police?"

"No"

"Well there's your answer then. Get to the bottom of it. Now tell me about this cyber attack?"

"Harriet would be better placed," said Denham.

"I don't want the detail, just who and why?"

"The who is easy, China. The why is proving more problematical? There was a murder at one of the labs on the science park in Cambridge, as you know, and it seems the Chinese have hacked in and taken out the CCTV."

"So for some reason the Chinese are covering up a murder?"

"That is the only obvious conclusion."

"What does this, what's the place called, Techmat Technologies actually do?"

"It doesn't seem to do much, research into materials," said Denham.

"There you have it, classic plot. Evil villains steal secret formulae from lab and kills scientist, followed by World domination cornering the market in the rare material."

"Good theory, it would help if something was actually missing."

Denham looked down at the folder he held. "There was nothing stolen, according to John Tatum CEO of Techmat Technologies."

"You can see why I didn't join the police force in any event."

******

"Pay attention all of you," DCI Harrington was addressing the team of Detectives in the incident room back at the Station. "I have split you into teams, DS Pemly will lead with the Huang murder investigation and DS Susan Miles will lead on the murder in the park. Let's start with you DS Pemly?"

"We were hopeful that the CCTV would give us an easy break. We requested the coverage for the night of the murder. It has been erased, all of it."

"Who erased it and when?"

"Computer forensics has gone all over it. The system was hacked and erased remotely. It seems to have been done while DI Harrington and I were on site, on the morning of the murder, asking questions."

"Pity we didn't take a copy when we were there? Anyway, we have the visitor log on the gate," said Harrington.

"No we don't. The visitor log is electronic and part of the system that was wiped."

"You are kidding me? Let's think. What about the security guard, who has interviewed him? He should be able to tell us who went in and out that night."

DC Evans stood up, "He seems to have gone missing. He has a flat in the old bit of town and I have been round, rang and left messages. No one seems to know where he is."

"For fucks sake, in other words we are nowhere in the investigation. Right, let's make this happen. You find this guard and find him soon. Circulate his details and let's see what he remembers. Pemly get this, what's his name, in charge at Techmat in here and see what he can tell us. Go to it."

Pemly gathered his team and headed off.

"Now DC Miles, tell me about this body in the park."

DC Miles stood up. "We have had no luck in identifying the deceased as yet. The forensics has come back with nothing, apart from the fact that the dog was killed first. It appears the dog was lured into the woods and killed, throat cut. The owner then must have entered the undergrowth looking for his pet, where his throat was also cut."

"How do we know the dog died first?"

"The blood, the victim's blood was on top of the dog's blood. Resetting the scene, it seems likely that the victim found his pet and was cradling it or leaning over it when he was attacked."

"Have we found the weapon?"

"No luck, we have done a fingertip search of the crime scene and nothing has turned up. We can say the knife was sharp. It cut through the fur, sinew and soft tissue of the dog's neck in one continuous motion. A kitchen knife would not be capable of such a clean slice for example. It would have taken several sawing actions to get through. Dog skin and fur is substantially tougher than the human equivalent."

"A hunting knife?"

"Or a military grade weapon used by the likes of the Special Forces, designed to kill."

"So our unknown victim could have been killed by an ex or current serving individual?" said Harrington.

"We obviously can't say for sure, but it is increasingly looking like this

35

was a planned attack and not just a random act on dog walkers."

"Any luck with witnesses?"

"We have the woman who found the body, but she saw nothing out of the ordinary. We are canvassing the area and will be in the Park tomorrow at the approximate time of death, to see if we can pick up on regularly dog walkers at that time."

"Was the victims DNA on our database?"

"He doesn't seem to have a criminal record. We are checking other databases but no hits so far. He had no, ID, wallet, phone or anything that might help identify him. We have to assume that the killer took it with him. It may be a robbery. If we identify him and his killer uses his credit cards, we might get lucky that way. But at the moment, we are stalled."

"Was his clothing any help?"

"Cheap supermarkets clobber, nothing bespoke that would help. Even his watch was removed. The killer knew what he was doing and has given himself as much time as possible to put distance in," said Miles.

"Find out who he was."

Chapter 9

Ban Dan's offices in Delhi were less than impressive situated in an unassuming office block. Ban Dan was a major player in the Global market place with interest ranging from steel to shipping, truck and car manufacture, to insurance. Who actually owned it was hard to determine, but it was a private company and remained within the family. Today, Gilroy Jones had a scheduled appointment with the Executive Board, with responsibility for the Companies Steel business around the World.

"Good luck," Charlotte had wished him, as reception phoned to say that the Hotel Rolls was waiting at his disposal. "I shall move our stuff to my chosen authentic Indian holiday bed and breakfast while you are out doing your millionaire deals. I will meet you back here and you can check out when you get back."

"Do we have to? I am quite happy here?"

"Listen, you will soon be a dad, then for the rest of your life you can do safe and steady. Too much luxury has just isolated you from the real World. Trust me, being part of real Indian life will be far more rewarding than being wrapped in a bubble and kept at arms length. Trust me, you will thank me."

Gil doubted that he would, but Charlotte was determined so there was little point in arguing the point. In any event, he needed to concentrate on the matter in hand.

"Please come with me Mr Jones," said the rather ferocious looking woman who appeared in the waiting area outside the Ban Dan board room. He rose from his seat and followed into the room. There were five men sat around a large table with twenty four chairs arranged around it.

The Board members were clustered at the far end. It was apparent he was to sit at the extreme, opposite end of the vast table facing them. It was a ploy to make him feel isolated and awkward. The people facing him were obviously used to negotiating and would use every little advantage they could to get an outcome that suited them.

There was a difficult period of silence Gil, opened his briefcase and removed the relevant paperwork. No attempt was made by the others present to ease the tension. There was no welcome and no offer of coffee. They waited, looking at him. He was to be in the spotlight. He was to make his pitch and they would be the judges.

Gil was not, however, in the least intimidated. He was seasoned in negotiations and knew the rules of the game. He had not clawed his way to where he was without his own brand of determination and application. He took his time and spoke with confidence.

"Good morning Gentlemen," he was greeted with an appropriate reponse from the Board. "I am here, as you know, to make and offer for your controlling interest in the Ban Dan steel works Port Talbot."

The man sitting directly opposite Gil, a very long table length away, responded. "Are you sure it is for sale?"

"Only you can answer that, but, as I am here, I have to assume that it is a distinct possibility. If I am mistaken, I shall obviously save both of us time and get on with the rest of my stay in your fascinating Country."

There was a brief moment of silence that was finally interrupted by a large smile, "Please continue."

"I have been steadily growing my interest in steel over the past few years. I ship and broker it, buy in bulk and distribute. I feel that the next logical step is vertical expansion into the production."

"An odd choice, demand is low, prices are low and the Chinese are overproducing and dumping steel at below cost."

"And the Ban Dan works is beset by labour problems," Gil countered.

"It is however turning into profit."

Gil ignored the last comment. "The Ban Dan foundry is a modern facility and adaptable. It produces a high quality steel and is one of the few suppliers. It is in a niche market place. The Chinese are not equipped to produce this type of steel."

"You seem to be making a good case for us not to sell, Mr Jones?"

"Gentlemen, I am realistic and I do not doubt that you are fully aware of the advantages you have. However, there is was big disadvantage. Is there not?"

"The Workers Pension Fund," came the reply.

"The shortfall in the Pension Fund to be more precise, it has a hole in it as big as the North Atlantic Trench. Is that not correct?"

"There are issues and that is the cause of the unrest among the workforce."

"I estimate there is a deficit of around eight hundred million UK pounds," said Gil.

"It is falling."

"I am prepared to assume the liability, guarantee jobs. The place is in chaos at the moment with the strikes and potential customers will lose confidence the longer it continues and ultimately the order book will decline and it will lose money again. The pension deficit will not go away."

There was a brief discussion among the Board members sotto voce. They then all sat staring intently at Gil before the Chairman spoke. "You have our attention Mr Jones. We are naturally puzzled as to how you think you can make it a worthwhile investments where others, including Ban Dan, have failed?"

It was Gil's turn to smile. "Well, if I told you that you would not sell it to me, would you?"

"Probably not, Mr Jones, so cutting to the chase, as they say, how much?

"One British pound"

"The current profit is under two million. It will take you four hundred years to recoup your money?"

"It is a brilliant offer for you is it not? I am guessing that the best you have had so far is a minus figure. I heard a figure of half a billion required by any new owner to take it on. Minus five hundred million off the top line of the Ban Dan group, in addition to the billion or so you have already had to write off on the original purchase cost. I am offering to take it off your hands and you walk away with no further liabilities," said Gil.

They knew he was right. The Chinese were the only other interested party and they required Ban Dan to put aside four hundred and fifty million pounds for them to do the deal. The industrial unrest was worsening the situation daily. "We have to ask ourselves what you know that we do not."

There was a short silence before Gil responded, "I am just an optimist,"

"We will refer it to the main Board with a recommendation to accept the offer."

Gil left feeling elated. The biggest deal of his life, he could not wait to get back and tell Charlotte. Even staying with an Indian family to experience real life, as she termed it, did not seem that bad after all.

He smiled as he thought of his final reply. One thing he definitely was not was an optimist. What he was, was the man who had attended Uni with Dr Stanley Huang, the real brains at Techmat. The new industrial process would make them kings of steel and he had that process in his possession.

He would not have been so happy had he seen the reports, in the press of the murder of Stanley Huang.

Chapter 10

"Wake, time to go home," said the custody Sergeant.

Reese Williams woke with a start and was completely confused. "Where am I?" he asked as he struggled to understand what was happening.

"You are in the nick my old son," replied the Sergeant, "and it is time to go home. We are releasing you on Police Bail."

"What time is it?"

"It's two thirty in the morning."

Williams came to full consciousness and cognisance. He had been released from hospital earlier that day and arrested. He had been charged with affray and kept in custody pending further charges. "Fuck! Can't it wait until morning?" he moaned irritably.

"We need the cells, matey. Get a move on."

He was given his shoe laces and belt. Having managed to replace his shoes, he was taken to the front desk, where he stood bleary eyed, facing the policeman. "Right, here's your property." He was handed back, keys, wallet, change, watch and a mobile phone."

"How I am I supposed to get home?"

"Phone for a taxi," came the reply.

Williams turned on his phone. The battery was flat. "There is no battery."

"Oh dear, what a pity, I must have left it switched on," said the sergeant.

"Can I make a phone call to get a cab?"

"Fuck off. You had your mandatory call when you phoned your brief. Looks like you will have to walk home, doesn't it?"

"Bastard," responded Williams. He was not surprised that the Police were being less than helpful, he had, after all, bashed one of them. He headed to the exit.

"See you soon," the Sergeant called as he walked out into the cold night air.

It was close to three in the morning on a week night. The Town centre was deserted. He started his walk to the mini cab office. It was less than a mile, but he was stiff from the beating he had sustained during the demonstration at the Steel works and his progress was slow.

He rounded the corner at the end of the road and as he crossed the deserted street, he became aware of the presence of others. He had not expected to come across any other living souls at this time of the morning.

He tried to hasten his pace but his right leg, in particular, was heavily bruised and he found it difficult to move faster. The street was darker than would have been the norm a few years earlier but, in a bid to save money and balance the budget, the authorities had resorted to turning half the street lights off after one o'clock on week nights. Williams was aware of the presence of a number of individuals waiting in the shadows of the doorways that lined his route, but he could not make them out.

Looking behind him, he missed the figure that appeared from an entrance way and stood before him until it was too late. Without warning, he felt a jarring pain as he was struck. He was knocked backwards onto the seat of his pants. He heard the footsteps approaching from behind and knew that he was about to receive, what is referred to as, a good kicking.

He knew he had been set up. The police were not about to let some one take a free shot at one of their own without a bit of payback. He was not surprised that the desk sergeant had looked so smug. He had bailed him at this time to ensure there would be no one around to act as a witness. He had made sure he had turned his mobile phone on to run the battery down, so forcing him to walk.

Williams tried to struggle to his feet and face his attackers. He was pushed back down and surrounded by his three assailants. They wore balaclavas pulled down to cover their faces so ensuring he would be unable to identify them. As in most towns, there was CCTV cameras everywhere, but for some reason the operator had pointed all of them in another direction. Nothing would show up if and when the footage was examined.

He rolled up in a ball and covered his head with his arms. There was nothing to be done and he waited for the kicking to commence.

The darkness was broken by the headlights from a lone vehicle turning into the road. The Astra van seemed to appear from nowhere, its headlights illuminating the scene, a lone man prone on the pavement surrounded by three men about to administer a beating.

Williams could hardly believe his good fortune. Port Talbot had as much life on weeknights as a graveyard after the Second Coming. It almost felt miraculous as the headlights rounded the corner and the van drove towards them.

"Fuck," said one of his assailants as the van stopped. "We have to get out of here." They ran from the scene as the van stopped yards away. Williams realised that they were not fearful of the lone good Samaritan that had stopped to investigate, but that it had not been part of their plan to assault innocent passers-by. That would have been too awkward.

"What the fuck is going on here?" said a Northern Irish accent.

Williams got to his feet. "Just an attempted mugging. Thanks, you saved my neck.

The Irishman got out of the van and made his way over to where Williams was struggling to his feet. He reached down and extended his hand, Williams grasped it and pulled himself to his feet.

"Jimmy McIntyre," said the man. "You look like you have already been in the wars. Not your week is it?"

"Reese Williams, I have had better I must admit."

"Do you live far?"

"About two miles away," said Williams.

"Get in, I might as well give you a lift."

"Don't you have to get back home or something?"

"As it happens I don't. For tonight you are looking at my home," he pointed at the van. "Get in and I'll tell you about it."

They pulled up outside Williams' flat. "So there you have it. I drove all the fucking way down here and find the fucking bitch is shacked up with another bloke. So I end up with fuck all in my pocket and nowhere to kip. I was going to park up somewhere, get my head down and see if I could get a bit of work on the morrow," finished McIntyre.

"Listen as you done me a favour I'll do you one. You can kip on my sofa for what's left of the night, if you want?"

"Are you sure?"

"Why not," said Williams, "and who knows, might just have a bit of work for you. There is a bit of a struggle going on at the Steel works and you look like you can handle yourself"

"This calls for a bit of a celebration," he retrieved a holdall from the back of the van and a bottle of Irish whisky "I thought I would be celebrating with a sexy lass tonight but I guess we might as well celebrate a new friendship."

Chapter 11

"To what do we owe the honour of this visit?" asked Tim.

They were gathered in the conference room in the basement of Thames House. Those present from MI5 were Tim Burr, Harriet Shaw and Harry Denham. Those present from the Defence Science and Technology Laboratory (Dstl) were the Parliamentary Under Secretary of State John Maitland and Shirley Mount.

The Dstl is a trading fund owned by the Secretary of State for Defence. It is funded mostly by the Ministry of Defence. The Government carried out a Strategic Defence and Security Review in 2015. One consequence of the review was the creation of a Government-backed initiative to help small and medium-sized businesses bring new innovation to the market place. In 2016, it was announced by the Defence Secretary, that the 'Defence and Security Accelerator' would have access to an £800m innovation fund and build on the 'Centre for Defence Enterprise' model, operating within Dstl.

Shirley Mount opened the conversation. "As you are doubtless aware, we are charged with pushing innovation in small companies?"

Tim responded in the positive. "What particular area brings you to our door?"

"We are interested in steel and in particular a small company in the Cambridge Science Park called Techmat Technologies. We have taken a sizeable stake in the business and were hopeful of dramatic developments."

"On the steel front, we have started to have a look at the recent unrest at the Ban Dan in Wales. You will have to expand on Techmat Technologies," said Denham.

"We have held an investment in the research there for a number of years. The key player and brains was a Dr Stanley Huang. The structure and finance was organised by John Tatum. He added the commercial knowledge to the equation."

"I think we need a little more detail as to what they were doing at Techmat," said Tim.

"A bit of background might be in order," interrupted the Under Secretary.

"A few years back Stanley Huang was undertaking his PhD into certain composite materials, including carbon ferrous, titanium and various ceramics."

"Not a clue," said Denham.

"It is not that important. What is important is that he worked out, in theory, a very lightweight and very strong material which should, if capable of being manufactured in sufficient quantities, have multiple defence and commercial applications. "

"Would you give us an example so we can get an understanding of its use?"

"Currently tanks use something called Chobham armour. Like most modern armour it is a composite with layers of different materials, such as plastic and ceramics. It has the advantage of being lighter than its metal equivalent but also takes up more volume. That is to say, it is bulkier so, its use is often restricted to the most important areas. There are less bulky composite armours, but they are prohibitively expensive to manufacture."

"Dr Huang discovered an alternative?" asked Tim.

"He did and he didn't. He found a way of using traditional ferrous based products and altering the structure to give it more integrity. In other words, he found a way of modifying steel to make it more bullet proof but only in the lab."

"Let me guess, he set up Techmat to develop the idea?"

"Almost, he first joined up with an old friend, a Gilroy Jones, also a metallurgist who had branched out in a different direction. He is a sort of steel mogul and deals steel around the globe. They started working together, but it was soon apparent that Huang needed a totally different set up to bring the product to the commercial stage. When Huang met up with John Tatum, Techmat Technologies was born and Jones and Huang parted amicably and remained friends."

"I can work out the rest. Techmat approached you and the necessary funded was forthcoming to develop the armour," said Harriet.

"Sort of, but not quite that simple, it was a lot more complex. But you are right in that we have a very keen interest in the product and more importantly, who has access to it."

"What is so good about it then?"

"It is thirty percent less bulky and twenty percent lighter than Chobham. More to the point, it theoretically would be half the price to produce than equally performing composite armour. Can you understand the implications?" said Shirley Mount.

The question was greeted by silence by the three MI5 personnel." Please continue," said Tim.

"Just imagine the impact it would have. The weight reduction would allow, for example massive fuel savings. Tanks do not do many miles to the litre. Their range would be significantly improved, resulting in millions being saved. But tanks are not the only things to need armour, ships, troop carriers and rocket launchers are but a few items of military hardware that would benefit. Further, the export earnings are also potentially game changing."

"And what is the link to Ban Dan works in Port Talbot?"

"Put simply, it is one of the few functioning steel works in the World that is still running and has the necessary infrastructure for manufacturing the new armour. We know from our last meeting with Dr Huang that he had cracked the production method to mass produce the new armour and its commercial potential was on the verge of being realised."

"Now the picture is becoming clearer. We have some evidence that there is an attempt to disrupt the Ban Dan works. GCHQ has been tracking the communications of the strike's leader, Reese Williams. He is being motivated by a foreign power. We are working to get to the bottom of it," said Denham.

"We do know with some certainty that the security systems at the Science park in Cambridgeshire, where Techmat Technologies is based, have been the subject of a cyber attack. It has the sticky fingers of the Chinese all over it," said Harriet.

"And of course, Dr Huang is now the subject of a murder inquiry by the Cambridgeshire Police," added Maitland.

"More to the point, there is no trace of the plans Dr Huang had just completed."

"Summing up, we need to find out what is going on at the Ban Dan works and find Huang's industrial process," said Tim.

Chapter 12

The Parliamentary Under Secretary of State - John Maitland and Shirley Mount left Tim, Harriet Shaw and Harry Denham contemplating the situation. "What progress have we made in Port Talbot?" asked Tim.

"Our man going under the name of Jimmy McIntyre has made contact with Reese Williams, the leader of the strikers at the Steelworks," said Denham.

"How did you manage to get him in place? It is a pretty close knit community and I assume the local police have tried in the past to get someone in undercover?"

"Apparently he was released from the local nick, where had been charged with as many things as they could think up, after he bashed one of their own. It seems that as he walked home, he was set upon by some muggers and our man, Jimmy, saved him from a kicking."

"That was a bit of a coincidence wasn't it?" said Harriet.

"I am guessing that it wasn't a coincidence ,but I am hoping that it wasn't MI5 agents doing the kicking?" said Tim.

"Give me some credit you have been in this game long enough to ensure that we don't get caught bashing random members of the public," said Denham.

"So who then?" said Harriet.

"Old bill, they were only happy to help."

"Well let's see what Jimmy McIntyre can find out and in the mean time, we need to monitor how the Cambridge Police are getting on in getting to the bottom of Dr Huang's murder. In particular we need to find that formula for that tank armour or who has it," said Tim.

"Let's hope it is not the Chinese," said Denham.

******

Leaving the meeting, Harry Denham headed down and out of Thames House. He checked his watch and realised he was running late for his luncheon appointment. He stood outside looking for a black cab. Being lunchtime, that proved problematical, but he was eventually seated and moving in the heavy traffic towards the Strand and Covent Garden.

His resentment of Tim Burr was well known in the Department and well known to Tim. Tim had leap-frogged him to the head job at MI5. Denham knew that the job should have been his when the former Head, Elaine Wilkins, died. He had more years seniority and was manifestly better qualified. Somehow Tim had support from the Cabinet. He knew not how or why this support came about, but he suspected there was some hold that Tim had over one or more of the members. He had been trying to get to the bottom of it but, so far, he had discovered little of any value.

Denham's digging had not been totally in vain. Three Russian tycoons had been killed in North London by, unlikely as it seemed, a bomb manufactured by an ISIS fundamentalist Islamic group active in Syria and Iraq. Just before their deaths, the MI5 undercover agent, acting as their Chauffer, had been pulled and a limousine put at their disposal was delivered to another person, as yet unidentified.

The police anti terrorist investigation could only get so far. Tim had resisted any inquiry into MI5 or its actions claiming overriding national security interests. Perfectly correct and reasonable, putting MI5 personnel at risk was clearly not the job of the police. The investigation had tracked communications emanating from MI5 to the limousine provider, but that was as far as they could go without cooperation from the Agency and that was not going to happen on Tim's watch.

Denham had dug deeper and had followed up internally. He could not prove anything, but he knew Tim was directly linked to the phone call. Not enough to use in a Court of Law and certainly not enough to prove beyond a reasonable doubt but certainly enough to cause embarrassment. If handled correctly maybe enough to get rid of Tim Burr.

The Met or Scotland Yard coordinates and leads counter terrorism in the Country with forty-eight thousand officers, they are a formidable force. They are headed-up by the Commissioner who is supported by his deputy, Christopher Moon.

Currently Christopher Moon was looking at his watch in Rico's Italian Restaurant at the entrance to Covent Garden on the Strand. Denham had arranged lunch at the beginning of the previous week. They had been at Eton together and had maintained their relationship over the years, as do many old school chums. Their paths had diverged, career wise, but they kept in touch. Moon, like Denham had been passed over for the top job, in Moon's case this was the job of Met Commissioner. He, like Denham, was resentful of that fact.

He stood up and waved as Denham finally entered the restaurant. "Bloody traffic," said Denham as he sat.

They ordered pasta and the conversation started with the necessary pleasantries as to health and family. They both knew that catching up was not the prime agenda and they both knew that the discussion was not to be work related or their discussion would have been recorded in the minutes of their organisation. There was to be no record of this meeting.

"I think we may be in a position to help each other," said Denham.

"What are friends for?" said Moon.

"Exactly, we both seem to find ourselves in the same unfortunate situation. We both seem to find ourselves working for a boss that, quite frankly, is not up to the job."

"Well mine isn't. That is for sure. He likes taking the credit and the honours but hasn't known a decent days work in his life."

"Well, I have in this envelope a morsel of information that you may not be aware of. Something that was dry cleaned from his record when he was vetted for the job," said Denham.

Deputy Commissioner Moon sat more upright and put down his fork. Denham held his interest fully. "Go on," he said.

"When Gilmore, the now Sir Gilmour head of the Met, worked in Northumbria and he was a lowly superintendent, he was friends with a local bigwig Councillor, same Masonic lodge, nights out and even a few shared family holidays."

"So what is the significance?"

"I have been using MI5's resources and GCHQ to dig into everything about your boss. This Councillor, friend to the local police, has been investigated wheny they were looking into historical child abuse. He was a friend and a governor at a number of children's homes."

"I am aware of the case," said Moon.

"But are you aware that Superintendent Gilmore sidelined an investigation twenty six years ago into his then friend?" He passed an envelope, taken from his jacket pocket, across the dining table.

"What can I help you with?" said Moon as he pocketed the envelope.

"It is more that I may be able to help you with an inquiry that is up against a brick wall."

A second envelope passed across the table. "This contains enough evidence linking my boss Mr Burr to the bombing in Highgate, in which the three Russians died, to cause a scandal, not enough to prosecute, but enough to request an Official Inquiry into the affair, just enough to cause a major scandal if it got out."

Moon took the envelope and it joined the first. He smiled, "A toast to, hopefully, our rapid promotion."

"To promotion," Denham raised his glass.

Chapter 13

"He is in the interview room," said D, Pemly. It was two thirty in the Police Station in Cambridge and DCI Harrington had finished lunch half an hour earlier. As they were finishing their cups of tea, a uniform had collected John Tatum, CEO of Techmat Technologies and brought him to the Police Station.

The two detectives took up their seats opposite, Tatum and Pemly opened the file on the murder of Dr Huang. Harrington would make the running and ask the questions.

"You are not a suspect and are merely here to help with our inquiries," began Harrington.

"I am not really sure I can help. I have very little more to tell you, other than what I told you at the Office."

"I am sure you want to do everything in your power to track down the killer of your friend and colleague Dr Huang?"

"Of course I do. It is truly dreadful."

"Quite so and any small detail you can remember could be the piece of information that brings his killer to justice. So let us start at the beginning. Start with the last time you saw Dr Huang."

"It must have been around half past five, quarter to six. I had just finished a phone call to a business contact in the States. I usually wait until the afternoon to phone the US because of the time difference."

"Do you have the phone number and name so we can get an accurate time?" Tatum pulled out his phone and read off the details. Pemly made a note.

"Please continue," said Harrington.

"I came off the phone and tidied my desk, put my coat on and locked the door and left. Going downstairs, I called in on Dr Huang who was still working in the lab and said goodnight."

"Was he on his own? What about the other people who worked alongside him?"

"He was on his own all day. Normally he works with his team of three researchers and a lab technician. There was a lecture taking place at the Uni. He had given them the day off to go. It was more a mini symposium and the three PhD researchers were keen to go. The draw was professor Turgev, the renowned physicist. They all really wanted to get the chance of seeing him in the flesh."

"What about the lab assistant?"

"Huang gave him the day off."

"So the last time you saw Dr Huang was around six o'clock?"

"That's correct. I left him working. You could check the exact time of the log at the exit gate, all coming and goings are recorded."

"How did you get home?"

"The bus that runs past the park and then I walked home."

"Did anyone see you?"

"Lots of people I suppose, including the driver of the bus but no one I know."

"Did you go straight home?"

"I was tired and I had something to eat and stayed in, watched some TV and went to bed"

"The next day?"

"I have, more or less, fixed routine. I got up at six and arrived at the Science Park around eighty thirty and found the police there."

"Again, did anyone see you?"

"Not to my knowledge."

Harrington looked at Pemly. "Is there anything further you would like to ask?"

"No, that about covers it," came the reply.

"Thank you for coming in. We may have further questions but that will do for now."

Tatum was shown out by a uniformed constable and Harrington and Pemly sat facing each other across the interview table. "Doesn't get us much further, does it?"

"Can we confirm any part of his movements?" asked Harrington.

"Nothing inside the park as the CCTV has been hacked and wiped clean. The gate log is also wiped and the barrier guard has gone missing."

"How about the bus and the driver?"

"We have spoken to all the drivers on or about the time. None can be sure of seeing him or not. He is a regular traveller so it is a case of having seen him but not sure if it was then or the day before."

"Were the busses equipped with cameras?"

"None on board, not worth the expense on the country routes, the troublesome passengers tend to be in town and late at night usually."

"So we have no evidence proving or disproving his statement. What about his phone call to the States?"

"Checks out and the three researchers alibis are water tight."

"That leaves the lab technician."

"No it doesn't. Her alibi is cast iron as well."

There was a knock on the door and DC Miles entered. "Sorry to interrupt but you need to see this."

"What is it?"

"It is the forensic report on the dead. Nothing new, but the victim has been identified."

Pemly looked at the report, "You are kidding me, aren't you?"

"What is it?" asked Harrington.

"The body with the dead dog, it is Matthew Watling, the guard at the entrance to the Science Park, identified from his dental records."

Harrington sat quietly thinking. Running the facts through his mind, the CCTV destroyed, the gate log missing, no witnesses, Tatum, the last to see the victim alive and now the guard murdered. He had a dead man and no clues to the perpetrator, except for a report of a possible Chinese link to the hack of the security systems.

The who was difficult but the why, the motive was plain, the industrial process Dr Huang had perfected. It was obvious that who ever had killed him had taken the details of the process. "What about the computers?" he asked Pemly.

"There was nothing missing from the lab, Tatum confirmed it," said Pemly.

"No, not the physical equipment, is there anything missing from Dr Huang's computer or database?"

"How would we know that? We are looking for something that is not there?"

"No, we are looking for something that was removed from his computer and downloaded or copied and then erased. We are looking for any event that occurred after his time of death and the body being discovered by the cleaners."

"I am not clear," said Pemly.

"Let us assume the motive is the plans stored on Huang's data base. We know that Huang is highly tech savvy and we can assume that his computer is, to all intents and purposes, un-hackable. So, if you wanted the process, the only way you could get your hands on it was to get Dr Huang to give it to you. Or more simply, all you would have to do is wait for him to log on or be logged on and then physically access his computer. So let us assume that Dr Huang is working in his lab with his computer on."

"I see, the perpetrator kills him and takes what he wants from the computer and then erases all traces of his work," said Pemly.

"Then you remove all evidence of your being there by hacking the CCTV and killing the only witness who can identify you."

"Get his computer forensically examined and it will tell us the exact time he was killed."

Chapter 14

The family in Delhi welcomed Charlotte into their home with a floral garland placed around her neck. A red dot was placed on her forehead by Sami while Eshan, her husband, helped carry her and Gil's luggage in. The house was pleasantly but plainly furnished, in contrast to the opulence of the room she had just vacated at The Leela Palace. The smell of fresh bread and curry leaves pervaded the house and the noise from the street could be heard through the open windows that provided a fresh breeze throughout the house. Charlotte felt she might miss the air-conditioning at the Leela. She had checked her travel guide and knew, however, that the mosquitoes would not yet be breeding, owing to the cooler temperature at this time of year. One thing less for Gil to moan about she thought as she followed Eshan up the stairs to their bedroom.

"All of Indian life is here. We are giving the full Indian experience," smiled Eshan as he placed her and Gils luggage in the corner of the room. "As you can be seeing we have full five star facilities, toilet, bathroom and electricity. You can charge your computers in your room or be using the electric razor."

Eshan's comments reminded Charlotte that both her and Gil's tablets needed charging. They had used them on their train journey and forgotten to plug them in at the Leela the previous night. "I shall take you up on that," she said and taking both from their protective cases inserted the chargers. Nothing happened.

She looked at Eshan,"We are having electricity, but Delhi is not always having electricity. Sometimes it likes to take a well earned rest then it comes back vigorously."

Steel

Charlotte laughed "power cuts?"

"Indeed, power cuts but soon you will be charging," he confirmed. "No please to be following your esteemed host to the rest and relaxation facilities," he gestured for her to continue up the stairs. At the top of the stairs was a heavy wooden door which she was urged to push open.

She stepped out onto the flat roof of the building surrounded by a low parapet wall. There were chairs, rugs, cushions and a low table arranged in a neat circle. There was a bottled gas fired cooking ring surround by pots to one side and a line draped with washing that ran cross the rough and was tied to the adjacent building.

"First a warning," said Eshan. "The running of electricity cables is an art form in Delhi and these cables should be avoided at all costs by the uninitiated. As you are seeing, these cables and wires run like intertwined snakes from one building to another. People make their own adjustment, adding wires as needs be, so please to be very careful in coming into contact with them."

Charlotte looked out across the roof tops. There was as much activity up here as there was in the streets below. Cooking, washing clothes and bathing were taking place all around. She was fascinated by the sight. Vivid colour was all around. The omnipresent mist that pervaded Delhi at this time of year had burnt off with the arrival of the sum and the sky was an unending blue. Saris of all colours hung from washing lines, walls were painted in all the colours that could be imagined, shines, symbols and painted statues of the Hindu gods all added to the vibrancy that assailed the eye.

Charlotte stood there for a while taking in the sights and sounds of India. Eshan stood quietly waiting for her to finish her viewing experience. She realised that she had been looking for sometime and looked at her watch. "I need to get back to the hotel to get Gil," seeing the time. Can you get me a taxi?"

"Oh very certainly," said Eshan as they made their way down the staircase. "But I am providing the full chauffeur service for a small additional fee. I have a fine car and I am having the full insurance. I can be hired to transport guests day or night to wherever they are wanting to be going."

She had agreed and found herself sat beside Eshan as they drove back to the Leela Hotel, where she was to collect Gil on his return from his meeting with the Ban Dan Executives.

The driving experience was something that no person brought up on the roads of the UK could be prepared for. Cars, bikes, lorries and the omnipresent three wheeled tuk-tuks were playing a constant game of dodgems. Intermixed, in the highway mayhem, were horse drawn carts, wedding parties riding horses, rickshaws, motorbikes and camels carrying loads, all seemingly about to collide.

As they headed straight towards a motor bike with four people sitting on it, driving on the wrong side of the road, if there were such a thing, Charlotte said, "how do you know how to avoid a crash?"

"We are not knowing. It is Karma. If I am driving on the wrong side, if we crash it is my Karma to do that day."

"But what about the people you crash into, you could kill them."

"Only if it is their Karma," Eshan replied.

Charlotte admitted that there was logic. Bad driving was not the issue if Karma or your fate dictated that you were to die, then there was little to be gained by obeying the traffic laws.

Karma was clearly favourable to her that day as they arrived at the Hotel in one piece. Eshan parked the ancient car opposite. Charlotte checked her watch, Gil was due in a few moments. He had texted on leaving his meeting at Ban Dan.

The Rolls Royce with Gil in the rear was in fact only a few moments away from its destination. He was feeling elated at agreeing a price for the Port Talbot works. He had tried phoning Stanley Huang but had been unsuccessful. He wanted to share the good news.

He had the process that Huang had perfected and between them they would be able to provide the arms industry with new armour, lighter and cheaper than anything currently on the market. They had Government backing from Dstl, they would have the production capability and Stanley would be able to walk away from Techmat Technologies and, more importantly, out of the clutches of Techmat's boss John Tatum.

Gil could wait to tell Charlotte, even if it meant sharing in her authentic Indian experience in some bed and breakfast. The car was approaching the entrance to the hotel and glided silently to a halt. The chauffeur stepped from the car and opened the door for him, the Hotel doormen being engaged in other door opening activities with newly arriving guests.

He stepped from the car and thanked the driver. He looked around for Charlotte and thought he spotted her across the road in what appeared to be an old jalopy.

She saw the Rolls pull up carrying Gil and began to waive to attract his attention. On the corner, a uniformed police officer was talking to a man of Chinese appearance. "That is our esteemed head of Police, Reyansh Dutta," Eshan pointed to the pair, "He is a very bad man but also a very powerful man. See, he is taking money from that Chinese man. The Chinese are very powerful here. They invest and make massive trading with Indian companies."

Charlotte watched as the Police Chief walked away and directed some officers to stop the traffic. Gil spotted her in the car and waved. He started to cross the road, now devoid, briefly, of traffic.

The next few seconds were like a horror film. As Gil was in the centre of the road a lone motor bike appeared. The Chinese that had been talking to the Police Chief only seconds before, ran to Gil and appeared to push him. The motor bike pulled up, he jumped on the pillion seat and the bike disappeared from the scene. Gil fell to the ground throat cut and dying.

The Police Chief signalled to the officer on point duty to resume the flow of traffic, as Gill bled out, the road filled with traffic obscuring the crime scene. The Police Chief stepped into his waiting car very much richer and was driven off.

Chapter 15

"Listen up everyone time for a case review," said DS Pemly.

"Right! Let's have and update, start with the cell phones," said Harrington.

"Dr Stanley Huang made no calls on the night of his murder but he had made numerous calls to a Gilroy Jones. We checked Jones out, he is a close friend and a well known industrial entrepreneur."

"What line of business is he in?" asked Pemly.

"Steel"

"OK, possible suspect material, he would want the process Huang was working on," said Harrington.

"Not necessarily, he was a close friend. They could have been working together commercially," said Miles.

"So no phone calls from Huang before his death. What about the location?"

"His phone did not move from the lab."

Miles continued, "We have checked Tatum's phone log and location. There is nothing of significance."

"Run through it anyway," said Harrington.

"There is nothing to run through. He is in the Techmat offices until around six pm when he said he left."

"Then you tracked the phone to his home."

"No, it is switched off until the next morning when it is switched on at Techmat, presumably when he returns to work."

"And the body is found," said Pemly.

"So we have no idea what he did the evening Huang was murdered, apart from his statement. No CCTV at the Science Park, no witnesses on his journey home and the gate log has been destroyed and the gate guard murdered?"

"Have all the potential witnesses been interviewed who were in and around the Science Park that evening?"

"All the other businesses have been checked out and their employees. No one saw anyone come into or leave the park after six pm that day. It does mean not someone did not enter the Park or go to the Techmat Technologies offices, kill Dr Huang and leave with the plans. But it does mean that there were no witnesses," said Pemly.

"This is not making sense. Has forensics come up with any thing on Huang's computer?" asked Harrington.

"Nothing at all, in fact, apart from looking on social media, there was not any activity all day. No files were copied or removed. The only activity was that evening when the whole system was examined."

"What time was that?"

"A period of some three hours commencing at around six fifteen," said Miles.

"Well that narrows the time of death, somewhat. The Killer arrives on the Park sometime after Tatum leaves around six. Huang, we have to assume is killed by six fifteen and the killer searches his computer for the plans. Clearly they are not on the computer and he leaves empty handed. We have to assume that the Chinese are behind it as the computer systems and CCTV is hacked and wiped clean. GCHQ is virtually certain that the Chinese carried out the hack. The only loose end that needs clearing up is the gate guard Matthew Watling as he is the only person who has seen the killer arrive at around six pm after Tatum has left.. The killer then follows Watling and kills him and his dog the next day when he is exercising the dog in the park near his home, said Pemly.

"So we are looking for one killer for Watling and Huang?" said Miles.

There was silence and the detectives looked at Harrington. "Have we spoken to this Gilroy Jones?" he asked.

"That won't be possible. He was in India on business and was caught up in a street mugging and was knifed. He died on the street outside his hotel."

"That is a big coincidence isn't it? Are we sure it was a random mugging?"

"I have contacted the Police chief, Reyansh Dutta and he has confirmed it was just one of many muggings in the City. They are investigating the matter."

Sitting in his office, Harrington looked unsettled. "What is it?" asked Pemly.

"I just don't buy the whole thing. Bring Tatum in. I have an alternative idea how this went down."

"I can't see any other way the murder could have been committed," said Pemly.

"Well I can, how about the following scenario?"

Chapter 16

"So here is my theory," said Harrington. Pemly pulled up a chair opposite his boss' desk.

"I don't see what other theory fits the facts?"

"Let's examine the facts shall we? The cleaner comes into Techmat Technologies office to start work at approximately six in the morning and finds Huang dead. Is that correct?"

Pemly nodded as he read the statement. "That's clear from the statement."

"Then Tatum arrives first on the scene and together they phone the police?"

"The call from Tatum's mobile is logged at the Police Station at fourteen minutes past six."

"When was his phone switched on according to the mobile provider?"

"At exactly eight minutes past," replied Pemly.

"Now look at the bus times that morning and the GPS on the busses. There is one bus that arrives at five forty and the next arrives at six ten. Is that not so and did they not both run exactly on time according to the GPS on the buses?"

"I don't see?" said Pemly.

"Look at the timings, according to Tatum he arrives just after the body is found. So he must have caught the bus that arrived at five forty am.

He could not have caught the one arriving at six ten as his phone is in Techmat and switched on by eight minutes past six. The bus is still two miles away at that point."

"So he caught the earlier bus."

"So it takes a few minutes to get to the office so where was he from five forty until eight minutes past six?"

"There is a missing half hour," said Pemly.

"Look at the statement of the driver of the bus that arrived at five forty."

Pemly found the relevant point and began to read. "The bus was running on time and I arrived at the Science Park at five forty. I did not actually stop as there were no passengers waiting at the stop and no one wanting to get off."

"Tatum was not on the five forty bus nor could he be on the six ten bus. So how could he be in the office to discover the body with the cleaner at around eight minutes past six?" asked Harrington.

"I don't understand," said Pemly.

"The obvious answer is that he was already there."

"How could that be?"

"Look at the evidence. We can not find witnesses that saw him leave the previous evening. We can not track his phone because it is off. The bus drivers cannot remember seeing him. There is no evidence that he ever left."

"What about the security guard and the CCTV?"

"Let me run through what I think happened. Tatum comes off the phone to the US as he says in his statement and we confirmed. He then goes to the lab and tries to get Dr Huang to give him the plans for the industrial process. A row develops. It escalates and Tatum kills him. He examines the computer and finds that Huang has already removed all traces of his work. He is now stuck with a dead body on his hands."

"So why doesn't he leave?"

"He is a clever man and has a background in chemistry. He knows if he goes home he will take trace evidence blood, Dr Huang's DNA with him. We searched his flat and it was clean, no blood, no transfer, no nothing. He waits for the cleaner to arrive and goes to the crime scene and gets the blood over himself. The cleaner sees it and for that matter also picks up blood."

"He cleans himself up in full view of the first attending officers," said Pemly reading their statements. It should not have been allowed, but they cleared the scene and he went to the bathroom where he openly washed the blood from his clothing and himself.

"What about the CCTV?"

"It was not destroyed to prevent us from seeing the killer arriving and subsequently leaving. It was destroyed to prevent us from seeing the fact that Tatum did not leave the previous evening. He killed Huang and just waited all night for the cleaner to discover the body. He just switched his phone off so his movements could not be traced."

So Tatum killed Dr Huang. Who killed Matthew Watling, the gate guard?" asked Pemly.

"Not Tatum that is for sure. But he had to have somehow organised it. I have checked his phone calls after we left. Something the team did not do as they had no reason to." He handed Pemly Tatum's phone records.

There, at seven thirty was a call. Pemly looked at who Tatum had called. It was to The Changpu Corporation.

Harrington continued. "Tatum phones a Chinese company, who it appears, and I have checked them out on the internet, are steel manufactures, just the sort of people that would be interested in Huang's industrial process. Then, before we can recover the security log and the CCTV, it is hacked by the Chinese and hey presto, all is wiped clean."

"Then someone kills Watling, the only witness that can say Tatum never left Techmat Technologies offices that night."

"Bring him in," said Harrington as the door opened.

"What is it, Miles," asked Pemly.

"There has been a body found with his throat cut. It is John Tatum."

Chapter 17

Du Longwei had lived in the UK since he was a child, his parents left Hong Kong before it was handed back to the Chinese in nineteen ninety seven. The British lease had expired and they were forced to leave. They had a presence on Chinese territory since the eighteen fifties.

The Chinese had always been a patient race and with a history of thousands of years, a couple of decades did not even register on the scale on their timescale. They planned for the long term. Du Longwei's parents were sleepers. Agents planted by the Chinese Government for use in the future, a long term play. He had grown up in England. He had been to school in England. He was British but he was not, if you peeled away the surface.

His parents had been successful and built up a restaurant business in China Town in London's West End, along with an import business brining in authentic Chinese ingredients. The business was always destined to be successful with the Chinese Government helping it to thrive. They never encountered any difficulties from the State in obtaining the necessary paperwork to ease the passage of their business with Hong Kong or mainland China. The business empire they had built was destined for success, the Chinese Government ensured it.

Du Longwei inherited a business empire and his parent's fierce loyalty to China. His parents had ensured that his loyalties stayed true to the cause. As Ignatius of Loyola leader, of the Jesuits, reportedly said, "give me a child until the age of seven and I shall give you a Catholic for life," so it was with Du Longwei and China.

The Triad gangs in London were available to him as muscle if he needed to call on them. The criminal gangs, notorious in Hong Kong, operated throughout the UK and had arrived here in the post World War II period. They operated prostitution, extortion and drug rings in most of the major cities. Their affiliations were in Hong Kong still and they operated with the forbearance of the State. While they were powerful, they were no match for Beijing. The State had the resources and the power to remove all trace of all and any that stood in its way. The Triads were useful and so were tolerated. They had been useful toDu Longwei in the past and would doubtless be useful again.

The drive to Cambridge was tedious but necessary. While the internet was an easy means of communication, he knew that following the recent events at Techmat Technologies and the death of Dr Stanley Huang, all communications would be closely monitored by GCHQ. Whilst The Changpu Corporation wanted the production process developed by Huang, it did not want to cause a diplomatic incident that could impact on Chinese trade. The murder of Huang had not been part of the plan, nor had the necessary cover up and subsequent murder of Matthew Watling, the guard at the Science Park.

Du Longwei had been sent to Cambridge to gain control of the situation. He would make sure he did.

The park was to be the rendezvous point. He sat and waited, watching the dog walkers. It was tranquil and so English. It was hard to contemplate that it had been the scene of the brutal murder of Watling. Oddly, the British press had been more appalled at the death of his dog than they had of his.

Tatum sat down on the bench beside him. "Do you have it?" said Du Longwei.

Tatum shook his head, "It was not there."

Du Longwei was shocked, "I don't understand?"

"It was not on his computer."

"But he is dead."

"It was an accident. It was not supposed to happen that way."

"An accident, Huang is dead. The security guard is dead. We have had to wipe the CCTV and entry log. You have forced the Chinese and The Changpu Corporation to expose its involvement and now you say it has been for nothing?"

"I approached Huang and reminded him that the process belonged to Techmat. He said that he knew that I intended to sell it to the Chinese. He was full of patriotic crap, saying our support and finance came from the Defence Science and Technology."

"Did you offer him the ten million pounds?"

"He just wasn't interested"

"So why is he dead?"

"It wasn't intended. It just got out of control. I tried to take his computer and he fought back."

"So he is dead and it was not on the computer?"

"I checked it, nothing, completely wiped clean. He obviously suspected my affiliation to The Changpu Corporation and he had taken steps to take it out of my reach."

Du Longwei sat silently contemplating the mess the whole affair had become. It had appeared so simple. Acquire the failing Ban Dan Steelworks and using Huang's plans produce the new lightweight armour. Now there were two deaths and everyone from the police to MI5 were looking at Techmat Technologies. "Where are the plans?"

"He has a friend, Gilroy Jones, they are close. He would have trusted him."

Du Longwei realised things had just gotten a whole lot more fucked up. Jones was at this precise moment lying in a morgue in Delhi. The Changpu Corporation had there rival bidder for the Ban Dan Steel works conveniently mugged and killed, leaving them the only other buyer in the race. Whilst they could buy the Steel Works for a song, now, they did not have the method to make the armour.

Longwei rose from the bench and walked from the seated figure of John Tatum. It was a crisp, dry day with a slight chill in the air. "The English countryside is beautiful, is it not?"

"I prefer the city. I'm not a great lover of fresh air," replied Tatum.

Longwei removed the black commando knife from his pocket and walked around the bench. "That saddens me. I was hoping that you would find peace in such beautiful surroundings. He walked behind Tatum. Bending forward, he grasped his hair and pulled his head back exposing his throat. He drew the knife slowly across his exposed throat. The blade was so sharp and the cut so precisely applied that Tatum had no time to react as the blood gushed from the cut that ran the full length of his neck. There was a small gurgle and a gasp for air. Longwei lowered his head back onto his chest.

The dog walkers and passers by passed the man sleeping on the bench not seeing the spreading red stain on the front of his clothing. Only when a curious dog, not on a lead, jumped up onto the bench and began lapping the blood was the corpse found and an ambulance called.

Chapter 18

Chunyun was in full swing. The forty day travel frenzy for the Chinese New Year would last until the end of February. Over three billion passengers were travelling back to their families and homes from all over China. Snow in many of the provinces had brought travel chaos and millions were waiting across the Country at rail stations, waiting for the tracks to be cleared and trains to run.

Wei Feng wanted to get back to his family and, being the head of the Changpu Corporation, he had a private jet at his command. The advantage of private air travel was nullified by his need to deal with the crisis facing the Company. His trip had to be put on hold as sat in the chuffer driven car, he waited in the log jam of cars blocking virtually all movement in Beijing. Meng Fan and Jin Jianjun were also struggling to get to the meeting.

The three Board Directors eventually reached the headquarters of the Corporation. The building was awe inspiring and excessive but spoke of the new confidence prevalent in China. It was a statement, a statement of permanence, of global presence and power. It rejected the old made in China brand, suggesting shoddy manufacture and spoke to the World of excellence. China was taking its place as a super power, a business force to be reckoned with and the Changpu Corporation was out in front, waving the flag and competing successfully with the best.

Wei Feng was the first to arrive in the Board Room. He stood looking out across the city, or at least he stood overlooking the cloud of pollution that cloaked the city. Millions were on the move for the New Year celebrations and he to would have liked to have spent time with his grandchildren but, for now, he had to deal with Company business.

Eventually all three arrived and were seated at the vast circular table meant to seat up to fifty people. Jin Jianjun spoke first. "I fear we are losing control of matters regarding our offer for the Ban Dan Steelworks in the UK. I have just received some disturbing news from Du Longwei."

"I thought we were on top of all eventualities?" said Meng Fan.

"That, as it turns out, could not be further from the truth. As you know, we had a business arrangement with John Tatum at Techmat Technologies to deliver to us the industrial process to enable us to manufacture a whole new form of steel armour. As you know, Mr Tatum became involved in an unfortunate situation that resulted in the death of his partner, Dr Stanley Huang."

"Surely Du Longwei sorted that mess out along with a little help from our Government?"

"That he did, killing the witness Matthew Watling while the CCTV was hacked and removed," said Jin Jianjun.

"So we have the formula and we have covered our involvement. Admittedly the murder of Huang was not supposed to have been part of the plan, but it has been dealt with and all we need to do is progress our bid for the Steelworks?"

There was a silence as Meng Fan chose his words carefully. "We do not have the formula. Tatum failed to mention, when he requested our assistance in clearing up the mess that he created, that he had not retrieved the formula from Huang before he killed him."

"Du Longwei has disposed of Mr Tatum and he will pose no risk to us."

Wei Feng was clearly angry as he spoke. "Where is and who has the formula?"

"We only have circumstantial evidence but it is compelling. Dr Huang's long term friend is Gilroy Jones, before Tatum was dealt with, Du Longwei established that they had maintained communication"

Jin Jianjun spoke, "and that explains the generous offer he made to Ban Dan for their interest in the Steelworks."

"That our spies in the Company inform us, they are minded to accept."

It was Wei Feng's turn to speak and entrust further bad news to the assembled. "Mr Jones has been the victim of an attack in Delhi and is dead. I, with the help of the Chinese Embassy and the Police Chief Reyansh Dutta, ensured that our competitor was removed from the field of play."

"Oh! That is brilliant. We have just disposed of our only possible link to the formula," said Jin Jianjun.

"It is a mess. I admit that, but there is still a way forward. Firstly, we instruct Mr Reese Williams, our paid agitator at the Ban Dan Works, to step up his activities. With Gilroy Jones dead we are the only buyers in the race. Let's buy as cheaply as possible."

"What about the formula?"

"Jones was in India with his fiancée. We need to obtain his laptop, tablet and other such devices and we need to question this Charlotte Carter. She may me able to lead us to where the formula is. I am sure Chief Dutta may be able to assist us in our quest."

Chapter 19

Charlotte was frozen in time and events seemed to move in slow motion. She felt detached. She heard screaming as from afar and then realised it was her screams. She opened the door of Eshan's car. She leapt from the car. She ran. She saw the road beneath her feet. Her feet seemed hardly to move. The seconds that passed appeared like hours until she reached Gil lying in the street, dying outside the Hotel.

She knelt beside and lifted his head. She frantically tried to stop the blood as it pumped from the jagged cut to his neck. She heard herself screaming for help. The crowd formed around them and seemed to be curious of the spectacle, detached, watching rather than offering any help. It seemed as though she and Gil were part of the street entertainment.

Gil looked at her and recognition was in his eyes. There was a resignation as to his fate and a dignity in the calmness of his loving gaze. She pressed harder with her hands, staunching the blood loss temporarily.

Time just stood still. She held him as he clung to life. They were saying their goodbyes in silence. In the brief moments they had left, everything that ever had to be said and everything that will ever be said, passed between them in that instant, a lifetime in moments and a loss that would last a lifetime for Charlotte.

The ambulance appeared from nowhere. How it was called and how it arrived would never be clear. It appeared to be on standby. Charlotte was grateful and cared little that the crime scene had been compromised and all evidence was obliterated. She was pushed aside as the paramedics set to work. Lines went in, oxygen mask on, blood staunched as the scene exploded into a flurry of activity.

Gil was ready to be moved. Barely clinging to life he was placed on the stretcher and loaded into the ambulance. Charlotte and the medic climbed in the rear with lights flashing they drove off.

Charlotte hunched over Gil, holding his hand while the medic monitored dials and gauges and watched oxygen and pain relief administration. Gil whispered and Charlotte leaned close. The medic was aware in his peripheral vision of an exchange of words between them and Charlotte retrieving an item. She lent down and kissed her man. The monitors alarmed and went flat.

She was pushed to one side as the medic began working on Gil. He worked furiously, but Charlotte knew that she had had her final moment with the man she loved. She had at least one thing that would endure. A part of Gil that would be there as a tangible reminder of him, inside her growing, was his baby. The tears ran down her face as the ambulance slowed and the siren and lights were turned off. There was no longer any urgency to transport the dead.

****

Terrance Mailer's fortunes had a major reversal for the good. Following his interference in MI6's operation, he had served a spell on the Back Benches. A new Prime Minister had seen all that forgotten. He now held the post of Foreign Secretary and the oversight of MI6. MI5 of course came under the Home Office.

Bernard Waverly's rise to head of MI6 had been on the coattails of Mailer. Neither men had any love for Tim but they had no option but to support him. Tim would forever hold the hilt of the Sword of Damocles that hung over the two men. He had in his files the dirty secret that could destroy them overnight.

The three sat in the Home Secretaries office. Mailer was talking, "Bernard has come across a piece of disconcerting information and I fear it may affect us all."

"It is not of any importance how I came into possession of this, but we need to deal with it. Your deputy, Harry Denham as I am sure has absolutely no love for you, in fact, I think it is fair to say, he loathes you. In his eyes you came in over his head and took the job as Head of MI5 from under his nose. He expected that job, he earned the job but you stole it away."

"Circumstances," said Tim. "Not in anyone's control put me there."

"True, true, tragic circumstances at that, with the suicide of Elaine, the previous Head. As you say, one has to be pragmatic. Keep things to ourselves and between the three of us. No need to rock the boat in these stormy Brexit times."

"Mr Denham is not merely rocking the boat, he is trying to sink it," said Waverly.

"I am not following," said Tim.

Waverly laughed as he pushed a copy of the Times newspaper across the table for Tim to read. "You don't keep up on the news much for someone one that heads up counter intelligence, do you?"

"Met Commissioner faces calls for resignation. Britain's top cop under increasing pressure to step down," read the headline.

"So," said Tim.

"So," said Waverly. "Denham has supplied his deputy, Christopher Moon, with the ammunition to shoot the boss, Sir Gilmour."

"I still don't understand? Why would my second in command, be interested in who heads up the Met?" said Tim.

"Oh I am sure he doesn't give a flying fuck," said Mailer. "He is interested in shafting you though."

"That is where my bit of intelligence comes into play. Moon is already paving the way to re-open the investigation into the deaths of the three Russians killed in that bomb blast in Hampstead, the bomb blast that seemed to track back to MI5, the self same bomb blast that, conveniently, killed the three pieces of scum who were responsible for your wife's death."

"When Moon takes over from Gilmour as head of the Met, which I am sure he will, you will be first on his case list," said Mailer.

"To be honest, I don't care if you are up shit creek without a paddle," said Waverly," but I would prefer it if we weren't in the canoe with you."

"I see, Denham has provided the ammo for Moon to shoot down his Boss and in return he has set me up as Moon's next target," said Tim.

"Time to get you thinking cap on and cover your arse," said Mailer.

"And yours, it would appear," said Tim.

Chapter 20

Jimmy McIntyre stood at the bar in the Red Lion in Port Talbot, about four miles from the Ban Dan Steelworks. "Remind me again," he called to Reese Williams and the other three steel workers sat around the table with empty glasses.

They had been drinking for a good four hours and mental capacity was beginning to diminish. Pint of beer had given way to shots of spirits. "Three whiskies and a pint," came the reply.

"I have that," said the barman. "What's yours?"

"A pint," said McIntyre.

Having been served, he made his way back to the assembled group. He had to make two trips in order to deliver the whisky and beer to the table with only minimal spillage.

"You are one of us now, congratulations," said one raising the whisky to his lips and taking a swing.

"Yeh , an honorary Welshman, even though you are Irish," said another.

"We forgive you, as we will beat the crap out of you in the Six Nations Rugby this year."

"You could only manage a draw last year," said McIntyre.

"You were fucking lucky. This year we will wipe the floor with you."

"The fuck you will," said McIntyre.

Williams had managed to wrangle McIntyre a job at the steel plant through his Union connections. He was still staying at Williams flat until he had a deposit to get a room elsewhere. They had developed a bond after he had saved Williams from the beating laid on by the local police.

McIntyre raised himself from the table and headed to the toilets having downed his pint. The toilet was empty and he entered the cubicle. Leaning over the toilet bowl, he put his fingers down his throat and emptied the contents of his stomach into it. His stomach was sore from the repeated heaving it had undergone during the drinking session. While the men around him were getting more and more drunk, he was still completely sober, albeit at the expense of his stomach. Being undercover, he had no intention of allowing a drunken slip of the tongue to raise any form of suspicion. He was well aware that one moment's lack of concentration and a casual out of place remark could blow the operation.

The other men drinking were less observant and assumed that Williams was matching them drink for drink. McIntyre spotted that Williams had been buying all the drinks at first. Going to the bar, he had ordered whisky for himself from the beginning of the drinking session. McIntyre had watched him empty his drink into the ice bucket under the guise of adding ice to the glass. Both men were feigning drunkenness. He knew his reason but he did not know Williams's.

As he left the toilet he could see Williams looking at the texts on his mobile phone. He rejoined as Williams hastily put the phone from view. Williams spoke, "we will really fuck them over tomorrow. Do we all agree?"

Another demonstration was planned for the following day. The three drinkers with Williams were his lieutenants and would be key in organising and coordinating the planned riot. They raised their glasses and cheered.

"That deserves another round." Williams got up and headed to the bar. He returned with double rations all round. "I won't be a tick. I just need to phone the ex." He left the bar and headed to the car park.

McIntyre made for the toilets. "That's the trouble with you Irish boys, weak bladders. Wait till we get you in Principality Stadium, Cardiff, then we will piss all over you."

He passed the toilet, both ladies and gents and headed to a door that led to the yard at the back of the pub. The door was unlocked, being designated as a fire exit. He crossed the yard, rounded the building and came into the car park from the opposite end from Williams.

At first he could not see Williams. Then he spotted him on his phone in the less well lit corner. He appeared to be talking into it while leaning against a sedan parked up there. McIntyre's eyes were becoming adjusted to the lower light level. He studied the scene and it was just what it appeared to be, a man leaning against an empty car making a phone call.

He was just about to leave and rejoin his fellow drinkers when something drew his attention to the scene. Williams stopped speaking and looked carefully around the car park. McIntyre retreated slightly into the shadow of the building as he glanced around to see if he was being observed. Satisfied he was on his own, he swiftly reached into the car through the passenger window and retrieved a packet that he quickly put in the inside pocket of the donkey jacket he was wearing.

McIntyre had, in the half light, completely failed to notice the open window to the car Williams had been leaning against as he mimicked talking onto his mobile. As Williams made his way back, he decided to wait and see who retrieved the parked car. He had his phone at the ready set to camera mode.

He had to wait a lot less time than he had expected. The light came on in the car's interior as the driver popped up and inserted the key in the ignition. McIntyre now realised that the occupant had been in the car the whole time. He had lain across the seats to avoid being seen. The phone conversation, supposedly being undertaken on William's mobile phone, had in actuality been a conversation with the driver. This had culminated with Reese, obviously being paid with the passing of the packet. It was clear that Reese Williams was a paid agitator at the plant and now, the indentity of his employer was the piece of information the MI5 man needed to determine.

The driver was framed in the cars illuminated interior. With his phone set to video, McIntyre filmed him as he started the engine and drove from the Red Lion. The video image was amazingly clear and he pressed the send button before erasing all trace of it from his mobile. MI5 were now in possession of the image of the man behind the unrest at the Steel Works.

Du Longwei, satisfied with his night's work drove cautiously, keeping to the speed limit so as to not attract unwanted attention from the police, back towards London.

Chapter 21

Tim, Denham and Harriet were in the operations room at MI5's headquarters in Thames House. It was seven in the morning but they had been working their way through the key issues confronting the Agency since six am. Unlike his processor, Tim liked to get things sorted early in the day, establish priorities, deal with the latest threats and set out policy and direction. He worked better in the morning having cleared his brain of distractions overnight.

The lone terrorist attack on soft targets had filled the first hour of their time. Along with the police, the antiterrorist unit, The Border Agency, MI6, the Transport Police, GCHQ and Special Branch it was an ever growing demand that stretched them all. The pattern that was developing both in the UK and the rest of Europe was difficult to counter. Individuals, often with only vague links to terrorist groups such as ISIS or Al Qaeda, were killing using low tech weapons - knives, cars or trucks. Often their only link to such radical Islamic groups was imagined. A personal grudge, a mental disorder or a need for self aggrandisement was sufficient inducement to go out on the streets of a major city and drive a car at pedestrians. Isis or a similar organisation would then claim responsibility for the actions of these deranged individuals.

These, lone would be murderers, were by nature the hardest for the security forces to detect and monitor. It was impossible to track, infiltrate or monitor everyone who was viewing extremist material on the web. It was even harder separating the fantasists from those that posed a real threat. The traffic on the web was monitored, but it produced too much information for all to be investigated in depth.

"We have had some success with the new algorithms in filtering the traffic to and from individuals engaging in dialogue on the extremist sites and networks. It is far from perfect, but we have been working closely with Psychologists and Psychiatrists in developing a more targeted approach. We are about a sixty per cent probability level of being able to sort the person that is likely to carry out an act of terrorism, from a pure fantasist that will just stay in their bedroom and talk about it," said Harriet.

Tim had pushed Harriet forward after her help in tracking down his wife and his best friend's murderers. She was only in her late twenties but had been promoted to head of the Cyber Counter Terrorism Division by Tim. MI5 now employed a large number of "quants ", quantitative analysts, much loved by Banks and hedge funds to develop algorithms to make vast amounts of money in the financial markets. MI5's object was not in making money but in spotting patterns and trends in terrorist activity.

"It is a bloody nightmare," said Denham. "MI6 have just announced an upping in the threat level, non specific of course."

"In truth it is not a matter of if but when. We are stopping attempts to kill or maim on a weekly basis between all the agencies, but inevitably one will slip through," said Harriet.

"We are improving and adapting. That is the key," said Tim. "What's next on the agenda?"

Denham clicked on his computer and the screens came to life with a video image. "This was taken last night by Jimmy McIntyre, the alias of our undercover agent in Port Talbot. It shows an, as yet unidentified, Asian male in his thirties handing a bribe to the leader of the strikers at the Ban Dan Steel works, Reese Williams."

He paused to check the file, "The information was passed to the West Glamorgan Police within hours. Extra police were called in overnight and the homes of all the identified ringleaders were   raided at around four am. All were taken into custody along with cash and details of secret bank accounts. Our man was taken in as well to avoid suspicion but will be released later, along any other innocents rounded up. Reese Williams will face a number of corruption charges."

"It is clear that The Changpu Corporation was running the show. I assume they hoped, by creating as much shit as they could, that they would make the future of the Steel Works so tenuous that it would leave them the only buyer left in the race?" said Tim.

"It looks like they are the only buyer in the race. Their sole competitor, Gilroy Jones, was mugged and killed in Delhi," said Denham. He projected the details of the Police Report of the murder onto the screen for all to view.

"That was a bit too convenient for The Changpu Corporation wasn't it?" said Tim.

"There is more," said Harriet. She removed the report of Junes death and replaced it with the report from the Cambridgeshire Police.

"Here we have three deaths connected to Techmat Technologies. As you know from our contact with State, John Maitland and Shirley Mount, at the Department of Science and Technology Lab, the key issue is the work being carried out into a new low weight, low cost armour by Dr Stanley Huang," she continued.

"Again, we come back to The Changpu Corporation. They would benefit from the research, especially if they can gets their hands on the Ban Dan Works in Port Talbot," said Denham.

"There are two further deaths, Matthew Watling, the gate guard and John Tatum," said Harriet.

"It's a bloody epidemic," said Tim.

"Two of the deaths, Watling and Tatum bear striking similarities, same location, a wooded area frequented by dog walkers and the same method, a stabbing. The weapon is thought to be the type of knife typically used by Special Forces"

"The death of Huang was blunt force trauma and doesn't fit the pattern, so a different killer?" said Denham.

"Correct," Harriet checked the paperwork in font of her before continuing. "The Officer in charge, DCI Harrington, sees it as follows. Tatum, the CEO of Techmat Technologies, tries to persuade or bribe Huang to make the formula for the new armour available to The Changpu Corporation and tell the Department of Science and Technology Lab that they have been unable to commercialise the process. Huang refuses and he his killed by Tatum in a struggle over Huang's computer. In order to conceal the death, the Chinese wipes the CCTV and kills the only person who can tell the police the comings and goings to the Science Park, Watling."

"So what is this Harrington theory regarding the murder of Tatum?" said Tim.

"Clearly Tatum failed to secure the formula. Huang had already removed it from the computer. Tatum had no value to The Changpu Corporation and was disposed of removing any link back to their involvement," said Harriet.

"That bring us back to Gilroy Jones's murder in Delhi," said Denham.

"As we have all worked out Huang, seems to have passed his formula to his old friend and former colleague, Gilroy Jones. So why kill him? "

"I think looking at the time line it was a cock up or it was truly a mugging gone wrong. I think The Changpu Corporation thought Tatum had the formula in his possession and they were removing the only other bidder for the Steel Works. I have contacted Ban Dan in India and they confirm they had agreed to sell to Jones' the Company just before he was killed. The probability is that The Changpu Corporation had a spy at Ban Dan. Seeing their chance of being successful in acquiring the Steel works they panicked and had Jones Killed. Bear in mind they had spent a lot of time and money fermenting discontent in Port Talbot using Reese Williams."

"It makes sense. Even with the formula, they would need to build a new plant capable of producing the armour. Even without all the red tape, environmental and planning laws that would slow such a project in the UK, it would still take five or six years before they would be ready to manufacture the new armour."

"On the other hand, if Jones acquired the Ban Dan works, his Company could be up and running in a year."

"So what is The Changpu Corporation's next move?"

"Get the formula?" said Denham.

"Except we don't know where it is?" said Harriet.

"It is most likely on Jones's laptop and the person most likely to have that is?" asked Denham looking at the files. "Charlotte Carter, his fiancée, who is still in India."

"We need to find her first."

"I'll get on it," said Denham as he got up and left the meeting.

Chapter 22

Tim spoke," I need to have a quick word."

Harriet sat back down as Denham left the conference room. "I am all ears."

"I had a meeting the other day with the Foreign Secretary, Terrace Mailer and Bernard Waverly, head of MI6. They have let me know off the record that I may be facing a few problems facing the deaths of the three Russians killed in the bombing in Highgate."

"I thought the investigation had been dropped."

It would seem that Gilmore is being replaced by Moon at the Met. Our own Harry Denham it would seem has had a hand in the matter."

"In what way," said Harriet?

"He provided the Moon with the smoking gun to dislodge Gilmore. As a quid pro quo, Moon will be coming after me with MI5 logs provided by Denham."

"He really wants your job, doesn't he?"

"Well it was never going to be a marriage made in heaven was it? I am only warning you so that you can get clear of the sinking ship. You have your career ahead of you. I only took the job to track down the killers of my wife. The rest was just a bonus."

"But you are actually brilliant at it," said Harriet.

"I know," laughed Tim. "Who would have thought it?"

"Surely you are not going to roll over and let that supercilious shit, Denham take your job. Are you?"

"You know as well as I that I am up to my neck in it. I am only involving you as forewarned is forearmed. Cover your arse and get clear before the shit hits the fan."

"I hear what you say. When will the old bill come knocking do you think?"

"A week or two I should think, that would give Moon time to get his feet under the table before he pays his debt to Denham."

"I'll give it some thought," said Harriet. She was getting up to leave when her computer dinged. She looked at the screen.

"We have identified our man in the Red Lion car park bribing Reese Williams. They have picked his car up on CCTV driving away from Port Talbot."

A photo of Du Longwei came up on the screen in front of Tim. "Du Longwei, British National with Hong Kong parents, he is known to us. He works for the Chinese. He has links to the Triad Gang in London. They seem to provide muscle when requested." The Triads were behind a great deal of criminality, mainly drug dealing, prostitution and loan sharking.

"He is the prime mover and shaker according to the police." A picture of a Chinese man in his fifties appeared on screen "Zhen Zhou, head of the 14k Triad organisation in London, They operate out of a restaurant in Chinatown in London's West End. Not someone you would want to meet on a dark night," said Harriet.

"I should like to know more about his links to Longwei," said Tim.

"How do you intend to go about that?" said Harriet.

"Fancy dinner tonight?"

"You have to be kidding," said Harriet.

"Organise a table at this Restaurant, the Flowering Lotus, for tonight."

"Are you sure?"

"Well book another three tables and have twelve field agents join us. It's about time MI5 indulged in some multicultural celebration, after all, it is the Chinese New Year."

"Talking of celebrating, its my birthday tomorrow. I am having a drink up at the Coal Hole on the Strand. Please come if you can."

"There you go then," said Tim. "What more could you ask as a present, a nice meal with your boss."

"I just hope I reach my birthday. Triads do have a bit of a bad press when it comes to bumping people off."

Chapter 23

China Town, in London's West End, was already heaving with tourists and the theatre goers finishing their pre-show dining when Tim arrived at half past seven. He drove his car into the car park beneath the Vale Royal House. Normally there would not be any chance of a parking space in China Town parking at this time of night but tonight was different.

He waited for the barrier to lift and drove down into the car park. The second level had been cordoned off. The signs were clear, "Reserved for festival organisers". The festival to celebrate the Chinese year of the Rooster was not due to take place for another week, but the explanation was good enough to explain to anyone looking to park not to raise suspicions.

There was an array of black transits already parked as he pulled into a space. The door to one opened as he got out of the car. Seeing Tim, the MI5 field agent recognised him. "Evening Sir, driving yourself tonight?" he asked.

"I can do some things for myself," joked Tim. "Is everything set?"

"Everyone is in position inside and out. We have conformation that Zhen Zhou is in the building and he will be going nowhere. The area is in virtual lockdown, a tick could not move here tonight without us containing it."

"Well done and remember, keep it low key," said Tim as he made his way into the pedestrian area outside. There was an air of excitement in China Town, a party atmosphere as the residents and businesses geared up for the main event, the parade to Trafalgar Square. Banners, streamers, flags and Chinese lanterns were everywhere. Lights blazed and even though it was a cold January night, the crowds were not deterred. The place was a hive of activity.

Tim struggled through the crowds to the Flowering Lotus restaurant. The front of the typical Victorian building had been embellished in the faux Chinese style. The door was guarded by two large Foo Dogs. They sat each side, made of stone, white and gilded in gold about a metre and a half in height. The glass window that looked out from the dining room to the street was etched with dragons and oriental lettering, wishing luck and happiness to those who entered.

The flowers that gave the eatery its name were carved in relief from a wood surround that engulfed the facade. Painted red and gold it truly was a statement piece. The whole demeanour of the restaurant told, the would be diner, that they would be paying full price to eat here. This place did not serve the usual sweet and sour chicken, it presented itself as fine dining with prices to match.

Tim looked through the window. He could see clearly the twelve MI5 agents inside finishing their meal. They had managed to obtain tables across the room from each other with the wall behind them. They had effectively set up a situation where they could all set up a cross fire for anyone in the centre of the dining area.

Tim looked at his watch. It was precisely eight o'clock. "I am not usually on time, but as it is work I thought I should make an exception," said Harriet as he looked up.

There was something different about her. Tim studied her for a while. After staring for a bit he finally solved it. "Have you changed your hair style?" he asked.

"A 'good evening Harriet you look nice,' would have been better," she said. "The colour, what colour is my hair normally?"

"Oh, you have gone ginger," he said.

"I like to call it bright auburn. However it could be mistaken for ginger by the less fashion conscious among us."

"Was it supposed to come out that colour?"

"Shall we just leave the matter now and go in. I am getting cold standing out here on the pavement."

Tim decided that he had lived dangerously enough and decided that he would be safer eating in a Triad run restaurant than criticising a woman's choice of hair colour. He stepped aside as he opened the door for her to enter first. They waited for the maitre' de to seat them.

"Mr Burr, table for two," he said.

They were shown to their table, given the menu and left to make their selection. The interior of the restaurant was no less ornate than the exterior. Red, gold and black dominated the colour scheme and dragons, foo dogs and lotuses the motif. The waiter returned after the requisite interval.

"Are you ready to order?"

"Please bring Mr Zhen Zhou to our table now."

The waiter looked surprised. "Sir we do not have such a person here."

"Just tell him to get down here, now," said Tim.

The waiter, whose job was to wait on table, looked confused. He was also frightened. He had no wish to go into Zhen Zhou's office and tell him to attend on a customer demanding to see him.

"Tim saw the hesitation. "Listen my friend, just do as you are told. Go up to the office and tell you boss to get his fat arse down here. It is quite simple."

The colour drained from the waiter's face as he hastily headed away.

There was a delay and two Chinese men appeared from the door leading to the private area. They marched across the dining room. These, thought Tim, were the notorious 14k foot soldiers famed for their up close and personal violence. Their preferred method was to hack their victims with meat cleavers or hatchets. Severing fingers, limbs and horrendous scarring sent out the message loud and clear. "Don't fuck with 14k."

Time watched as they crossed the room. They parted their suit jackets as they approached the table revealing the vicious looking cleavers in their belts. They stood, intimidatingly glowering at Harriet and Tim. "You don't come in here and disrespect Mr Zhen Zhou. Get up you piece of shit."

Tim looked up slowly and the thug was surprised at the lack of fear on his intended victim. Tim spoke. "My friend, you seem to have fallen foul of the old adage. You have brought a knife to a gunfight."

There was confusion on the faces of Zhen Zhou's henchmen. Then a voice spoke from one of the other tables. "I suggest you do as Mr Burr requests. He has a much bigger gang than yours. It is called MI5 and he is the head of it."

Fear now entered the two thug's minds as they saw the twelve agents, all with Uzi machine pistols drawn. "Oh, and please tell Mr Zhen Zhou to not try and leave the building by any other exit as it is surrounded by police marksmen."

Tim, Harriet and the twelve agents sat and waited. The Agents had aligned themselves to take down any hostile rush from the door the thugs had left by. The fears were unfounded. Zhen may have been a vicious gangster but he was not a fool. The door opened and he stepped into view. "I am unarmed and alone," he said as he walked to Tim's table.

"Please sit down," said Tim.

Zhen took a seat, "How can I help you?"

"I should like you help in a security matter. I need some information, that is all."

"I am not an informant."

"And I am not a policeman, I am head of this Country's Security Service and you are a British Subject. I therefore expect your full cooperation."

"If I don't?" said Zhen.

"I really feel that would be very stupid. As I said, we are not the police. Do you really want to make and enemy of me? I think that would be a very serious error. Don't you?"

Zhen sat quietly for a moment as he digested the consequences of having MI5 all over him. The Triads were not specifically targeted by the police. Their illegal activities attracted the same level of attention as the many other gangs operating around the Country. Their entrenchment in the Chinese community and its tradition of silence to outsiders offered them a slight advantage when dealing with their countrymen. A Security crack down would be a wholly different matter. Zhen was intelligent enough to imagine how his and his associates every more would be monitored. They would be put out of business.

"How can I help, Mr Burr?" he asked.

Tim produced the picture of Du Longwei. "You know this man, so tell me all."

Zhen did not attempt to lie or deny. "He is an associate. Some I must work with,"

"Triad member, a rival perhaps?" asked Tim,

"He is more in your line of work but for the mainland."

"He works for the Chinese Government?"

"Who he precisely works for or who he reports to I have no knowledge. It is clear that if you do not cooperate with him. very bad things could happen to people in Hong Kong."

"I see," said Tim.

"Harriet, would you wait outside for me and I shall join you in a minute." She looked puzzled but did as Tim requested.

She watched through the window as Tim spoke for a further moment. She saw Zhen write on a piece of paper that Tim took and put in his pocket before shaking hands and leaving with the twelve agents.

"Stand down Tim commanded," and the MI5 presence disappeared from the area.

She and Tim walked out of China Town and walked down the road away from the Shaftsbury Theatre. "I love the milk shakes in here," he said as they entered the burger bar. "I said I would get you dinner. What would you like, a double whooper with cheese is good?" he smiled.

Chapter 24

Gil had been pronounced dead on arrival at the hospital. Charlotte had stood by watching hopelessly as they tried to revive him. Today she has returned to the hospital to formerly identify the body. They had not let her see him when she was last here. It was too distressing to see your love one hooked up to drips and tubes and all the paraphernalia that was needed to attempt to sustain life. No one should have to carry the resuscitation attempts as the final memory of their loved one.

Eshan had driven in his old jalopy. The traffic had been as horrendous as usual. The delays provided Charlotte with a form of comfort. She would have stayed held up in traffic forever rather than come face to face with the reality. Now, looking at Gil as the mortuary assistant pulled back the sheet to expose Gil's face, there was no avoiding reality.

She let out a cry of anguish. Even though she knew he had died, seeing him in this place, all alone was almost impossible to bear. It just did not seam real. Her brain just did not want to accept that he was dead. His face was expressionless in death and his eyes were closed, but he did not look as though he was sleeping. She expected him to sit up and smile but of course he never would again. She tried to remember the man she loved when he lived.

She took solace from the joy they had shared a few short nights ago as they stood on the terrace with the fire burning behind them in the brazier, attended by the Nawab. Jaipur was filled with life before them and they were alive. She remembered the look of excitement on Gil's face as she told him the news that he was to be a father. Briefly she was happy then, the fact that he would never see his child live and grow dragged her back into grief.

Her thoughts were interrupted. "Would you confirm that the deceased is Gilroy Jones?"

"Yes," she replied. Her voice did not sound like her voice. Her brain denying its authenticity, it was futile attempt to deny the cold reality of death.

"Please be so good as to sign the formal statement."

She signed mechanically. Not reading or comprehending what was before her. She watched as the assistant covered Gil's face. She felt like shouting, "don't leave him here alone." She remained silent as the tears formed and ran from her eyes. She forced herself to turn and walk. The few steps to the double doors seemed a marathon. One slow reluctant step at a time she left, forever, the man she loved.

Police Chief, Reyansh Dutta was waiting in the corridor as she exited. "My condolences," he said.

She had seen. She knew. This man offering comfort was involved. She had seen the behaviour of the traffic police out side the Hotel. She had seen him organise it all. He had insured that Gil was isolated and an easy target for the assassin. For an assassination was exactly what had occurred. It had certainly not been a random mugging and killing.

Charlotte wanted to confront this man, to expose him, but she knew at this juncture she was powerless. She would need help to get her revenge. At the moment she was alone. She knew she had to bide her time. Eshan had warned her of the danger this man posed. When the Tibetans had demonstrated outside the Chinese Embassy when the Deli Lama had visited India, he had brutally suppressed it. They were ruthlessly beaten and dragged off. It was common knowledge that the Chinese were his paymasters.

"Thank you," she forced herself to reply as she headed out and away from this man.

"I know this is difficult but there are certain formalities. I assume you will wish to repatriate the deceased?"

"Of course I shall."

"The British High Commission will help you make the necessary arrangements."

"Thank you, I shall contact them."

"We will need to contact you with some paperwork. I assume you will remain at the Leela Palace hotel until matters are sorted?"

It was clear that the Police had not bothered to follow up on anything, that no investigation of any description was underway. The Police had not even checked the hotel where Gil and she had been staying. Had there been any checks Dutta would have already known that she had checked Gil and her out prior to his assassination.

"Yes, that is correct," she replied. She did not trust this man. She felt safer in his not knowing that she had moved to Sami and Eshan's. She walked past him and out into the fresh air.

She was in a daze as she felt the cold chill over the morning damp air hit her. She was still in shock of the brutal reality of her lover's death. She was walking but not knowing where. She became aware of a voice.

"Miss Carter, Miss Carter," the repetition of her name finally caused her to focus. The hustle and bustle of the crowded streets and the traffic noise suddenly assailed her senses. It was overwhelming and she began to sob uncontrollably.

Eshan took her arm and led her to his car. "Come, come, it will be alright," he said soothingly.

Of course he was wrong, it would never ever be alright again.

Dutta looked down at the text message that his mobile phone had alerted him to. He walked from the morgue and waved to his driver to pull across the traffic from where he was parked to collect him.

"Chinese Embassy he commanded."

The drive to the Chanakyapuri district of New Delhi was slow, but eventually the car approached its destination. They waited outside gate one and a Chinese official left and joined Dutta in the car.

"Drive," ordered the Police Chief.

They sat in silence until they were a few blocks from the Embassy, "Stop and wait here."

The two alighted from the vehicle and entered a small café. They were served by a very nervous individual as he recognised the Policeman.

"What is this about?" asked Dutta.

"It would seem we were a bit hasty in dealing with Mr Gilroy Jones."

"What's that you say, a bit hasty? He is dead."

"We were under the impression that we had in our possession certain information. As it turned out we did not."

"You are making no sense," said Dutta.

"Our contact in the UK was charged with acquiring the details of a certain industrial process. We thought the formula had been acquired. We were mistaken. It turns out that Mr Jones had acquired the formula and not our man."

"So?" asked Dutta.

"So we were a bit too quick off the mark in disposing of our rival in the race to acquire the Ban Dan Steel Works. We can only assume that Mr Jones has the formula with him here in India."

"Well what do you want me to do? I can hardly question him as to its whereabouts as you had me kill him, can I?"

"Please do not be sarcastic we pay you a lot of money for your services. The formula will be on his laptop or memory stick. We want you to acquire his computer devices and hand them to us. You will be well rewarded. Seize everything, bring it to us and we will take what we need."

Dutta was less than happy when he returned to the car and ordered the driver to take him to the Leela Palace hotel. He would have to be careful. Charlotte Carter was not the usual poor local who he could bully and push about. She was now the heir to a steel empire and wealthy. He had also learned from the conversation with the Chinese attaché that there were links to the Ban Dans, one of the wealthiest families in the World. He would have to tread very carefully indeed. He would not be able to bully his way past Charlotte Carter, she had the means and the contacts to make his life very difficult.

As he got out of the police car at the Leela Palace he resolved that he would not seek to obtain the computers, but would merely have an informal chat and hope he could gain access in some manner.

He approached the reception desk. "I should like to speak to Miss Charlotte Carter. Would you tell me which room she is in?"

The clerk clicked on the computer and examined the display on the screen. "Miss Carter and Mr Jones checked out two days ago."

Things had just got a whole lot more difficult for Chief Dutta.

Chapter 25

Tim pulled the collar of his crombie overcoat up over his neck as he made his way along the Embankment. The night air was crisp and clear. He sat down on the bench facing the Thames. He could see Westminster Bridge to his right and behind him was the Savoy Hotel. The clock on the hotel read five minutes to eight.

Looking down the River, he could make out the newest addition to the river's edge, the London Eye. The massive ferris wheel towered above the water and was brightly lit, the only star visible in the light polluted skies above the Capital. The various bend in the Thames prevented Tim looking further. If his view and his vision were infinitely better, he would have seen the iconic MI6 building, featured in so many "Bond" films, as it dominanated the river frontage at Vauxhall.

There had been plans to move MI5 into the Vauxhall building and free up Thames House but they had not been followed through on. Neither Intelligence Agencies had been keen on the move so for the present the status quo remained. Had the move taken place it would, however, have negated this evening's wander along the Embankment for Tim.

Bernard Waverly, Head of MI6, appeared on the bench at precisely eight o'clock. "It is a great City is it not? One rarely has the time to sit and appreciate it however. Don't you find?"

"Thank you for coming," said Tim.

"Always ready to co-operate, you know that."

Tim knew that to be far from the truth but now was not the time to dispute the matter. He needed this man's help. "I need a bit of a hand."

"That much I assumed. I also assume that you are, yet again, going well outside MI5's remit?"

"Old habits die hard."

"That is true, but let me stop you before we get into detail. I fear that you may not be in position much longer. How are the police inquiries going?"

"They haven't started yet. They will be in first thing Monday." It was Friday night.

"And?" asked Waverly.

"I fear they will not go well. My deputy, Harry Denham hates me. He wanted the job and he will have it whatever the cost."

"Yes, not a man of great ability but it would appear, one of great tenacity, well at least in bringing about your demise. Will the police find anything?"

"Unavoidable with Denham pointing the way," said Tim.

"What does he have on you, exactly?"

"Our own security measures work against me I am afraid. We, like MI6 and the other Government Agencies, need our phone network to be secure. The National Cyber Security Centre (NCSC), who are part of GCHQ, work closely with our own Cyber Team to ensure no one listens into our phone calls."

"Why would that be a problem?"

"It wouldn't normally, but it has the disadvantage during the encryption process of recording and logging which phone was used. If there was a beach of security it would tell us whose calls had been compromised, allowing us to limit the damage," said Tim.

"We all subscribed to the same protocol. Why is that such a problem?"

"There is one phone nobody else ever uses in our organisations, the most securely guarded."

"Yours and mine," said Waverly.

"Exactly, a phone call was made to a car hire company from MI5 that replaced their chauffeur with personnel from MI5. The car was subsequently used in an ISIS bombing killing three Russians. The driver and bomber were never traced. Tracing the call would obviously point the finger directly to MI5's involvement."

"And I assume directly at you?" said Waverly.

"I fear so," said Tim.

I don't see what I or MI6 can do to help? I am worried about certain matters pertaining to the Foreign Secretary and myself?"

"You have no need to worry and you can reassure Mr Mailer I will not be dragging him or for that matter, you, down with me. I shall keep my silence. I understand there is nothing either of you can do. The final matter is in the hands of the Police and the Home office."

"So putting it bluntly, why am I here?"

"Mailer is off tomorrow to pay the Chinese a visit. I was wondering if that situation might be exploited. I need a favour?"

Waverly realised, while Tim had just reassured him of his absolute discretion concerning the Foreign Secretary's unfortunate past, things could change. "Go on," he said.

"I would like to borrow your assets in China."

"Hold your horses. We have worked very hard over a very long time to get people in place. I have no intention of compromising them or risking their lives. You had better be pretty persuasive."

The conversation continued for a further fifteen minutes before the two men rose from the bench and made off. Tim crossed the road and made his way to the Embankment entrance of the Savoy. Passing the two uniformed doorman, he made his way up through the building, passing the various rooms with the hotel's links to Gilbert and Sullivan emphasised in their naming.

He eventually emerged in the lobby at the street level and the doors that led via the car turning area onto the Strand. He passed the Savoy Theatre where the night's performance had already started. He could see Covent Garden opposite, already busy with the night's drinkers and diners.

The Coal Hole was just on his left and he entered the crowded pub. It was packed, three deep at the bar and hardly room to stand. He managed to make his way past the bar and spotted Harriet and her colleagues in the corner. He noted they were mainly quants and programmers.

She spotted him, "Sir, thank you for coming."

"Happy birthday," he said as he squeezed through the crowd. "Let me treat you to a few bottles of bubbly."

He stayed for just over a half an hour. Having the head of MI5 at your party was slightly intimidating for the younger members of Harriet's guests. He took his leave when the group headed to Covent Garden where they had booked a meal at one of the restaurants.

He pulled his collar up as he walked down the Strand to Trafalgar Square. He felt alone. Since his wife's death, he often felt alone. He had avenged her, but that had not brought much satisfaction. Revenge was not sweet. He was still a man that lived but not complete. He knew that he could never be made whole again. As he stopped a taxi and set the destination for what had been their home in Muswell Hill, he realised that he was at the last roll of the dice and he was determined, that if Denham brought him down, he would at least make it a double six.

Chapter 26

"Come let's head over the road, we are already late for the booking," one of the girls in Harriet's party said. There were six of them left in the Coal Hole Pub, Harriet, Wendy, Christine, Mary, George and Kevin. They all worked in Harriet's department.

"I have to get back. The baby sitter goes at eleven," said Christine. "Have a nice time for me." She donned her coat and slightly, unsteadily left the pub to a chorus of "Goodbyes."

"And then there were five," said George.

"Four," said Kevin Drew. "I have to be in early."

"It's Saturday tomorrow, surely not?" said Wendy.

"It's the Police investigation that starts on Monday, I like to be on top of things."

Harriet made her way through the group and put her arms around Drew's neck. "I hardly know you. This would be a nice chance to get to know one another better."

Drew's complexion changed colour to match his hair, red. He had always been a nerd and freely acknowledged it. He was highly intelligent but physically unattractive. He had pale skin and his face was marked by acne scars. His teeth had not been a priority for his parents as a child and they were uneven and some crossed. To add to his lack of sex appeal was his poor physic, skinny and to finish it off, he had poor eyesight. Drew, it was fair to say had very little contact with the opposite sex in his thirty years on the planet. "Ok, I'll come," he said, still blushing.

Harriet kissed him on the cheek. "That's settled then. Let's go."

The group of five made their way from the pub and stood at the pedestrian lights waiting for the signal to cross. Eventually they turned to red and the traffic came to a halt allowing them to cross the Strand and make their way into Covent Garden. They turned left and headed in the Direction of the Opera House.

The area was packed with young people out for a good night. There were street food vendors lined up on their right, selling food from around the Globe as well as souvenirs of the tatiest variety. On the corner was a lone guitarist and further a street magician. There was a buzz about the place that drew visitors from all corners of the world here.

"This is it," said George, stopping at the entrance to a building.

The door had the mandatory large security guards blocking it. George spoke to them giving them his name. One of the bouncers spoke into the mike attached to his coat. Receiving confirmation via his ear piece that they had a reservation, he moved aside and allowed them access.

The party followed George down a flight of steps and were shown to a booth. Playing to one side was a loud band. Harriet sat on the inside with Drew opposite. Mary and Wendy shuffled along the bench and George sat at the end on the opposite side to Harriet.

The sound of the band made communication difficult. The server appeared and with a lot of pointing at the menu the order was placed. Drinks appeared first then more drinks. The restaurant was in no rush to serve the food. Drinks were where the profit lay and diners would be given as much opportunity as possible to order them.

Harriet looked at Drew and made sure he was aware of her gaze. She kept catching him staring at her when he thought her attention was elsewhere. She smiled at him encouragingly.

The food came. Essentially, the food was of the American variety, burgers and fries. The cost however was not. The food was priced at five times the Whoper Harriet had shared with Tim the previous evening in China Town. The menu description was of gourmet burgers made with one hundred percent beef and the chips were twice fried and hand cut. Harriet did briefly ponder what a beef burger could be made of other than beef and if the cheaper burger chains achieved their cheaper prices by having potatoes cut by people who used their feet rather than their hands.

Turning her attention back to Drew, who was sharing his enjoyment of his burger by eating with his mouth open, she casually allowed her clothing to become disarranged. She undid the top two buttons of her blouse. She did this after returning from the toilet where she had removed her bra.

On resuming her place on the bench opposite Drew, she also removed her shoes. She leant forward and made conversation with George, who was too far away to hear. She lent forward and made numerous vain attempts to engage in conversation. This was never going to be successful, but she saw from the corner of her eye that Draw was staring, mouth wide open and full of food at her nipples as her blouse parted as she lent across the table.

She smiled at Drew and sat back into the bench. She stretched her leg under the table, her bare foot found his leg. His trouser leg had slightly risen as he sat. She found bare leg and casually ran her soft foot up and down. Drew almost choked as he became aware that her bare foot was rubbing him. Harriet was striking, with firm breasts, pretty face and her recently acquired red hair. She was clearly out of his league and he was almost in a state of shock as she continued to slide her foot upwards.

Harriet was not stopping there. She half lowered herself under the table. Her shoulders were level with the top as she moved her foot further. Her bare foot gently came to rest in his lap. She moved it up and down staring directly into Drew's eyes. He was frozen with a comical look of ecstasy. She almost laughed. He looked like a dribbling fish as his mouth hung open and he took deep gulps of air.

She continued her gentle foot massage and she could feel his cock hard, pressing back through the material. Suddenly, she realised he was just about to come. She moved her foot away just in time to prevent an early end to her adventure. She realised that Kevin Drew had probably never had a woman touch his cock in his entire life. He was one of life's natural virgins.

She allowed him to calm down while still affording him the occassional glimpse of her nipples. The meal eventually finished and the group left the booth and gathered in front of the stage. George and Mary took the opportunity to get better acquainted and Wendy disappeared in the direction of the toilets with the girls she had been talking to for a whole six or seven minutes.

"Let's go." Harriet gave Drew no time to think and pulled him from the dance area and up the steps to the street above.

She pushed him backwards against the wall of the building and began to kiss him. She felt him tremble as she pushed her tongue into his mouth. He was awkward and in a rush. She felt like she was a school girl fumbling, not a fully grown woman. Drew was truly a virgin.

"Hotel," she said firmly and virtually pushed the stunned, overly aroused Drew along the Strand to the Palace Hotel. The receptionist was used to people turning up drunk looking for a bed, especially if they had struck lucky. They kept a number of rooms empty at about three times the price that could be booked online.

Drew allowed himself to be led to the room. Harriet felt as though she was dealing with a zombie. He was in state of shock. He could not have expected, in reality, to have sex with her. He had seen her in the office and fantasised an many occasions while masturbating in his bed. He had even masturbated in the toilets at work while fantasising about fucking her. The reality, on the other hand, was proving a bit overwhelming for him.

Harriet took charge and sat him on the bed. She removed her coat and then her blouse. He sat, trance like, just staring at her tits. She played it up and gently rubbed her nipples until they were stiff and erect.

He just sat and stared with his mouth open." Err, you need to take your clothes off," she said.

He continued to sit, staring at her tits. "Get naked," she commanded. The message got through and he managed to get undressed. She took his clothes and put them neatly on a chair.

"Watch." She commanded. He watched as she sat and removed her shoes. She still wore her skirt and panties but her breast and feet were bare. Pulling the chair forward, she sat and raising her legs gently lowered her feet onto his erect cock. Placing a foot either side of his penis, she gently rubbed up and down.

He was in raptures as she continued the foot job. Judging that he was in danger of coming she stopped. "Would you like to see my cunt?"

He mumbled something which she took as a yes. She stood and removed her skirt and the last of her underwear. She danced swaying in front of him exposing herself fully to his gaze. Drew had only ever seen a vagina in porno films on his laptop and once when he had seen a stripper at a friend's stag night.

Harriet slowed her dance, knelt in front of Drew and began to lick tip of his penis with her tongue. She inserted his penis fully into her mouth and sucking, slightly moved her head up and down. She completed no more than three strokes before she became aware than he was going to come. She stopped.

"I need to relax you," she said. "Lie on your front on the bed."

"She straddled him, her hand bag beside her. She opened the bag and removed a tube of lube." She started by leaning forward and slowly, with her tits resting on his back, rubbed herself up and down. He groaned and moaned as she continued to gyrate.

Her hands made their way to his anus. With a dab of lube she slid first one finger in. "Relax," she commanded. He breathed out and relaxed his sphincter. Slowly a second and third finger entered and she began to massage his prostrate.

It was six the next morning when Drew awoke. Harriet was dressed and at the foot of the bed. "Got to go," she said and without a second glance left.

Chapter 27

Eshan pulled up outside the British High Commission in Delhi. "Shall I wait?"

"No, I don't know how long I shall be," said Charlotte as she got out of the car. "I will phone and you can fetch me if that is OK?"

She stood there for a moment and hesitated. She did not want to go in. It would make it all so final. She knew she had to deal with the paperwork in order to fly Gil's body back to the UK, it would be the final acceptance of his death. He was never coming back and now all that was left was to tidy up.

She passed the policemen stationed at the entrance and made her way inside. She had expected a long wait, but was pleasantly surprised when a well dressed man in his thirties appeared almost immediately after she had announced her arrival. She followed him to a small well furnished office.

"Mr name is David Foal and I should like to offer you my condolences on your loss, I shall do my best to make the process as painless as possible, Miss Carter," he said. "Please take a seat."

The room was tastefully furnished with a desk at one end under the window and a coffee table with four chairs at the other. Foal had offered Charlotte a chair by the coffee table that had a pot and two cups already upon it. He gestured towards the tea. Charlotte shook her head in response.

"I do realise that this is a very difficult time for you and Mr Jones's family, but there are a few things we need to cover and a few forms to fill in."

"I understand," she said. Her voice cracked a little and she thought she would begin to cry.

Foal lent forward and poured the tea anyway. He handed it to her. It was too sweet but, it did soothe her slightly. It was not so much the tea drinking that settled her but the distraction the actual process created, the pouring, the sugar, the milk and the stirring.

"Take your time," he encouraged. "I shall try and complete as much of the paper work on you behalf as I can."

"It has all been so much of a shock. I cannot seem to get my brain to accept the reality. It was so sudden."

"We'll make a start if you feel up to it and see how we go. Do you have the death certificate?"

Charlotte felt the urge to cry again. She had an image flash into her mind of Gill lying completely alone in the mortuary. It was so cruel. She felt like leaping from her chair and going to comfort him, to keep him warm. She forced herself to reach into her bag and hand the certificate to Foal.

He carefully copied the details onto the form he held. The information could well have been entered directly into the system using the computer terminal which sat on the desk at the far end of the room. Experience had taught the staff that taking things down by hand was more personal and less traumatic for the deceased's relatives. The details could be entered into the system later.

"Have they released the body?"

It was hard to adjust. Gil had gone from being a person to a body. The question could have been phrased, "have they released him?" But the truth of it was in that question. Gil was now a body. She was arranging a box to be shipped back to England, no longer a passenger but cargo.

"I need to organise the collection. The airline was very helpful and provided the undertakers with the specification for the coffin, the law and regulations that were applicable." She had realised, speaking to the undertakers, that a death abroad was not an uncommon situation and they had dealt with many over the years. It had not, however, made it any the easier for her to cope with.

Foal continued with the questioning and eventually the paper work was complete.

"Will you fly back on the same flight?" he asked.

"I don't understand. Why would I not?"

"It is a matter of personal choice of course. It is that some people, especially if they are the deceased's sole relative, like to fly ahead."

"I still don't understand?"

"I am sorry. I just thought that you were Mr Jones' only contact in the UK. I understand his father his dead and his mother resides in Jamaica? I thought you might need to go ahead and organise the arrangements at the other end?"

"Oh, I genuinely had not thought about it? "

"I could help you deal with the airline and formalities should you decide to fly ahead and make arrangements." he said.

Charlotte sat in thought. She considered asking her Father to make arrangements, but she felt she did not want that. She wanted to organise it her way. To say goodbye her way, but she wanted to be with him and bring him home. She knew that it could not just be both ways.

"You are right," she concluded. "I must fly ahead. How do I go about organising it?"

David Foal was as good as his word. It was clear that the Commission, as well as the undertakers, had dealt with this situation many times before. He had the numbers and the contacts to hand. The only part she needed to be involved in was the payment and matters were complete.

"Is that all," she asked.

"Not quite," he said. "It is a very delicate matter, given the circumstances but I have been instructed to ask you some more questions."

"By whom?"

"I have been contacted by MI5. I know this is difficult but would you try?"

"Charlotte was confused. "We are not spies."

"Let me explain. Are you familiar with a Dr Stanley Huang?"

"Of course, he and Gil have been friends for years. They were working on something together."

"Have you read the newspapers recently?"

"No, I have been too distracted."

"This is very difficult indeed. I hate to be the bearer of even more bad news but Dr Huang was murdered."

"Stanley is dead?" she was shocked and felt as though the World was going mad.

"MI5 feel that Mr Jones and Dr. Huang's deaths are connected. I am not clear as to the detail, but I believe they were working on a joint venture that involved an industrial process and the acquisition of Ban Dan Steel in Port Talbot?"

"Gil was on his way back from a meeting with Ban Dan when he was murdered," said Charlotte.

I fear that you might also be in danger. It is likely that the same people were responsible for both deaths as well as a number of others. They are looking for the details of the industrial process to make a new form of armour. Dr Huang no longer had the process when he was murdered and MI5 believe he passed it to Mr Jones."

Charlotte said nothing.

"Do you know the whereabouts of the formula?"

There was a knock on the door and a young woman entered before Charlotte was able to answer.

"May I have a word?"

Foal got up from his chair and followed the young woman out of the door. He was gone some three or four minutes before he returned alone. His face was etched with concern.

"Things seem to be moving faster than we anticipated. There has been a warrant issued for your arrest. Police Chief Dutta is waiting outside and will take you into custody as you leave."

"I don't understand, arrest for what?"

"The murder of Gilroy Jones," he said.

"What," said Charlotte? "I had nothing to do with it. I saw this Dutta help the murderer to escape. If anything he should be under arrest, not me."

"There is a witness. He claims that you spoke to Mr Jones's murderer moments before he was killed. The witness claims that you gave this man money and then pointed out Mr Jones to him."

"It is all lies. It is not true. Who is this witness?"

David Foal looked at the piece of paper he had been handed by the young woman. "A fellow called Eshan, he drives you about apparently?"

"That cannot be true. He would not say that."

"He has apparently and the arrest warrant is legal."

Charlotte began to sob. None of it was making any sense. Only a few days ago she had been holding Gil in her arms. They had been so happy. She was carrying his child. Now he was dead and she was wanted for his murder.

"I need to seek instruction," said Foal. "There is one thing. Dutta cannot arrest you here in the High Commission. It is technically British soil and his warrant is no good."

Chapter 28

Police chief, Reyansh Dutta had his finger in every pie in the Chanakyapuri district of New Delhi. With in minutes of Eshan dropping Charlotte at the High Commission, he was informed. She had been spotted by one of the eight policemen he had stationed around the building specifically for that purpose.

Not checking the hotel had been an error. He could not have known that the Chinese would need to find her. Hindsight is a wonderful thing. The Changpu Corporation thought that John Tatum already had possession of Dr Huang's formula when they ordered Gilroy Jones's death. It had been a relatively simple idea but had spiralled out of control. Tatum was to steal Huang's process from Techmat Technologies. The Changpu Corporation would cause a bit of industrial unrest using the paid agitator Reese Williams at the Ban Dan Steelworks in Port Talbot and buy it for a song.

Instead, Tatum had killed Huang and failed to get the formula. The Changpu Corporation were then forced to cover up the murder which resulted in the killing of the security guard and Tatum in Cambridgeshire. Now, to cap it all, they had to find Charlotte Carter in the hope she knew where Gilroy Jones had put the formula.

Reyansh Dutta was not concerned with all of that too greatly. The Changpu Corporation's incompetence only meant one thing to him, a great big pay check to put things right.

"Detain him and find out where Miss Carter is staying," Dutta said over the phone to the Sergeant in charge of the police outside the High Commission.

Five minutes later he received a phone call back telling him that Charlotte was actually staying with Eshan and Sami at their boutique B and B. "I'll meet you there," said Dutta. "I am on my way."

He arrived to find Eshan and Sami handcuffed and seated on the floor in the living room. A search was underway. He waited patiently while the officers went through all of Charlottes personal items. "We have it," called an officer searching Charlotte's and Gil's luggage. He appeared in the lounge with a laptop.

Dutta made a phone call and they waited patiently for the computer forensic analyst to arrive. Dutta suspected that there would be no formula stored on this computer. Firstly it was not even password protected. He could see for himself, from the browsing history, that it had been used to look up facts about their trip to various parts of India.

More to the point, Dutta had the transcript of the police interview and of the ambulance crew that had come to Gil's aid and taken him to the hospital. The driver had very little to add to the investigation, but the paramedic that had travelled in the rear of the ambulance administering care, along with Charlotte, did have a great deal to reveal.

Whilst waiting for the arrival of the computer expert Dutta reread the statement of the paramedic. "I was monitory the patient's heart rate and oxygen levels. The young lady was holding Mr Jones's hand in a bid to comfort him. It was fairly obvious from our examination at the scene that the victim's chance of survival was negligible. The loss of blood was too great. I did notice that the lady bent close to hear what Mr Jones was saying. Following the exchange of words, the woman took something from the victem's inside pocket."

The paramedic was asked what the item was." It was a mobile phone."

Dutta was fairly confident that the formula that The Changpu Corporation was so desperate to acquire had been stored on Gilroy's mobile phone. He speculated that Dr Huang suspected that his boss was selling out to The Changpu Corporation, had done a deal with his old friend and colleague Gilroy Jones. Huang had managed to remove all trace of his work at Techmat Technologies and entrusted his work to Gil. Gil would strike a deal with Ban Dan in Delhi and between them they had, not only the method, but the means to produce the revolutionary new armour.

The forensic computer expert arrived and examined the laptop. It was as Dutta had surmised, it was devoid of anything of value or interest to The Changpu Corporation. He now had a problem if he were to get his payday. The formula was on the phone that was with Charlotte and Charlotte was inside the High Commission.

Now, in the normal course of events, this situation would have presented Dutta with little or no problems. Grabbing a local off the street and dragging him or her to police headquarters was routine. A bit of intimidation and a small amount of physical violence usually achieved the required result. Charlotte Carter was a wholly different situation.

The key difference was that she was rich and had powerful friends in the Ban Dam family. She was a witness and not a suspect. If he requested an interview, she would have the best lawyers and it would probably have to take place at the High Commission where he had no powers. There would be no opportunity to search her or her possessions. No possible way he could get his hands on Gil's phone and the formula. No way would he get the big fat payoff The Changpu Corporation were offering him.

Dutta knew that he needed a pretext to get Charlotte in his custody and relieve her of the phone. He made his way across the living room and sat facing Eshan. "I need you to make a witness statement," he said. "Tell me about taking Miss Carter to meet Mr Jones?"

"I drove Miss Carter to the Leela Palace and she waited in my car. She saw Mr Jones arrive in the Hotel's Rolls and started to make her way to join him. Before she got to him a man of oriental appearance attacked and stabbed him."

"I think you have forgotten something."

"No, I am being very certain in what I am seeing. I have missed nothing."

"Let me put it to you what exactly you saw. Miss Carter arrived as you said and you parked opposite the hotel. However, before Mr Jones arrived, she got out of the car and spoke to the oriental gentleman. You saw that she gave him a packet. A packet you had seen her earlier, in the car or at your house, she had put a great quantity of money. She then returned to the car where you waited until Mr Jones arrived. Then, as you say, he was stabbed by the man, Miss Carter had paid him to do so. Is that not the truth of it?"

"No, that is not the truth," said Eshan.

Dutta walked across to where Sami was seated." Hold her," he told a policeman. He grabbed her sari and the bra underneath and ripped it to her waist exposing her breasts. He started to massage the breast and nipple as he spoke again. "Your wife has a fine body and I think my men would enjoying taking it in turns fucking her." Turning to Sami, "you would like that. Would you not?" She struggled, but was held firm as Dutta continued to fondle.

"You are a very evil man," said Eshan. "I will not lie. I am a religious man, I will not damn myself or my family."

"Fucking religious fanatics," thought Dutta. "The County were full of mystics and zealots. They were always hard work."

He was pondering the situation when there was a sound from the hallway. "Papa, what is going on, where are you?" Eshan's and Sami's thirteen old daughter had just arrived home.

"There is a God," thought Dutta.

The girl was escorted into the room where she saw her parents handcuffed and her mother half naked. She began to cry.

"Your daughter takes after your wife. If anything she is more beautiful and of course a lot younger. I am sure my men and I will enjoy her far more. I shall spare your wife and we shall fuck your daughter instead, if that is ok with you?" said Dutta.

Eshan spoke. "I will sign your witness statement."

Dutta had the arrest warrant for Charlotte delivered to him as he waited outside the High Commission.

Chapter 29

The halls of residence were deserted apart from a few students who had no family to visit. The grey tower blocks that housed the students in Beijing looked even more depressing now, devoid of their occupants. The majority of the students had left to celebrate the Chinese New Year with their relatives.

Ling Ling pulled herself out of bed. It was lunch time. The absence of any family weighed heavily on her. She was usually a cheerful girl, just turned nineteen but New Year brought home the isolation. Her Mother had died when she was ten. She had not known her Father and her Mother hardly spoke of him. All she had told Ling Ling was that he had disappeared before she was born.

She had gleaned from her Mother was that they had lived in Hong Kong and when it was returned to China by the British, she and her Mother had moved to the mainland. She knew of no Grandparents or aunts or uncles, perhaps they were in Hong Kong. In any event her Mother never spoke of them.

She had tried to visit Hong Kong the previous year but was unable to obtain the necessary travel documents. It was then that she realised that she was subject to a travel restriction order. Not only could she not visit Hong Kong or leave China, she could not even travel in China outside of Beijing.

The restrictions imposed on her where usually restricted to political activist and sex offenders. The next grade up would have been house arrest or prison. She had tried to find out the why, but had been met by the usual bureaucratic brick wall. The more she delved for answers the less she learned.

She had put in numerous requests for her and her Mother's records, birth details, parents and grand parents. She had written to Hong Kong. She had filled in countless online forms. She was always met with the same response that no records could be found.

She pulled herself out of bed and went to the showers. The water was cold. The toilets smelt. The heating was off in the building. Ling Ling's start to the day was cold, lonely and miserable.

When her Mother died she had been sent to a boarding school. Now older that too was a puzzle, how could an orphan, from a poor single Mother and a missing Father, have afforded the cost of such an elite education. Who had paid the fees?

She had tried to find out ofcourse. The response had been that she had been identified by the teachers as a particularly able child and the State had granted her an education and maintenance scholarship. The only problem in that explanation was that she was not particularly gifted academically and in the incredibly competitive World of the Chinese education system, she would be ranked as an also ran. Despite her average results she had been offered a place at Beijing University, a scholarship and a bursary.

Her good fortune seemed to know no bounds. In December she had received a letter from the Civil Service saying that she was to be employed in the Ministry of Agriculture or some such. In fact, she had been enrolled in their University Sponsorship Scheme and they would pay her while she was studying. Upon the completion of her course, she would take up employment with them. She took the money, but still could not understand how she had obtained a job she had not even applied for?

Finally dressed, she realised food was becoming and issue. She looked around for something to eat. Apart from some noodles, the cupboards were devoid of anything remotely edible and the noodles had been there for several months in an opened packet.

She put on her top coat and cap. She pulled the flaps down and covered her ears. Looking from the windows she could not see the pedestrians on the streets below because of the smog and mist. She had lived in Beijing long enough to recognise a damp, cold day even if she could not see what people were wearing. She added a scarf left her room and started the long descent down the endless staircase to the ground.

The halls had been built in individual blocks and surrounded a square on three sides. Looking up, the tops of the buildings were shrouded in mist. It looked more like a prison complex than a place to house students. It was classic Communist Architecture. It's austerity contrasted severely with the newer buildings in the now rapidly modernising Country. Global brands had been attracted to China with its vast market. Old established residential areas had been cleared. People dislodged, mostly without any form a compensation, to make way for the spectacular and modern flats and offices.

All over China there was a new order. The elite were buying property and prices were high and unaffordable for most. There is the super wealthy, well connected and increasing international and outward looking. A wealthy, middle class of professionals is also thriving, serving the fast growing Global businesses. The mass of the population comprises the young, travelling to the city to find low paid work and the rural areas, populated by the elderly stuck in subsistence farming. The Chinese are proud of their ancestry and the Han people consider themselves better than others. Representing over ninety percent of the population, they discriminate heavily against the minorities, creating a deprived underclass.

Ling Ling started her walk to the local shops and stalls. There was a popular noodle bar where the students often gathered. The food was cheap and plentiful. The dual carriage way that passed the front of the Halls was unusually free flowing, a consequence of the mass migration to the rural areas to celebrate the year of The Rooster with relatives.

The Mercedes was parked on the forecourt of the car dealership a mile and a half from the halls of residence. The driver sat patiently with his cell phone on the seat beside him. His two passengers, both men in their thirties, had got out of the car and walked to the Halls several hours earlier.

The two men watched as Ling Ling crossed the quadrangle and continued her walk in search of food. The men had positioned themselves at opposite ends of the pavement. It made no difference which way the students walked as they exited the buildings, they would pass close by to one of the men. They, in turn, would get a good look at the faces of the students.

They were cold and bored when Ling Ling emerged. She passed the man. He double checked the photo he held and signalled his colleague. They caught her up and maintaining a reasonable distance, phoned the driver in the parked car. He started the engine pulled onto the road and headed slowly towards the three making their way along the pavement.

The car spotted the group of three. Ling Ling was slightly ahead of the two men as they all walked towards the car that came to a stop. The two followers speeded their space and caught up to Ling Ling, flanking her. They grabbed an arm each and lifted her feet from the ground. She found herself being carried along the pavement towards the car.

They dragged her into the car before she hardly had time to realise what was happening. Wedged between the two powerfully built men in the back of the car, she was unable to move as the driver sped off.

Chapter 30

"MI6 have just issued a warning to all our Embassies that they suspect the cabin crew of a major carrier have been infiltrated by a terrorist cell linked to ISIS," said Harriet as she entered Tim's office.

"How exciting," said Tim.

Harriet was puzzled by her boss's flippant reaction. "You seem less than concerned, given the severity of the situation?"

"No, no of course I am concerned."

"You don't look it. I am worried that we have not had a whiff of it. Nothing we have suggests any organised terrorist attack on an airline. Not a whiff of anything. No unusual internet traffic. Nothing is happening or planned. I don't get it."

"You must have missed something," smiled Tim.

"I miss lots of things, but this is not one of them. You know something, what is it?" said Harriet becoming annoyed with his smug attitude.

"All will be revealed," said Tim.

"Fuck you," said Harriet as she left his office, slamming the door behind her.

Tim laughed and picked up the phone. "Get me David Foal at the High Commission in New Delhi."

There was a short wait while he was located and came on the phone. "Foal speaking," said the voice.

"Hello, it is Anthony Burr here. I need you to do something for me."

The conversation was brief and then Tim made his next phone call. This time to the Chief Executive of British Airways, "My name is Anthony Burr and I am the head of MI5.I need your cooperation in a matter of National Security. I shall be contacting all the major carriers and asking them for their support as well."

Having obtained the help of the major airlines, he then made a final call to Bernard Waverly. "Tim here, I just want to thank you for your help in issuing the airline terrorist alert. Did you manage to approach the Foreign Secretary in helping in the other small matter we spoke of? I understand he has left to meet the Chinese President in Beijing already?"

Reassured Tim sat back in his chair and drank his coffee.

****

Charlotte Carter had settled into life in the High Commission in Delhi. She accepted that she was stuck while Dutta had the place surrounded, waiting to seize her with his trumped up arrest warrant. Consideration had been given to issuing her with a diplomatic passport and affording her Diplomatic status, making her immune from prosecution. The Government was unwilling to go down that route. There were protocols to follow and no one wanted to breach them. In nineteen eighty four a young police woman had been shot by staff inside the Libyan Embassy in London. Protestors had gathered outside and shots were fired from the Embassy, resulting in her death. The Libyan Government exercised their right to diplomatic status for their staff that allowed the killer to leave the UK unhindered. Now, the majority of states waived this right in the case of serious offences.

Foal joined Charlotte as she sat in the apartment provided for her." Hello, we have a busy day today. Firstly, we have organised a hair appointment for you."

"I don't want to appear ungrateful, but, just because I am a woman, a hairdo is not the solution to all my problems. What next, a trip to buy some shoes?"

He smiled," I assure you it is not sexism. There is a good reason for you to have your hair done. Secondly, I need you to change into a different set of clothing."

****

The MI6 security alert was causing disruption to flight schedules but in the main, passengers were understanding to the need to guard against terrorist threats. The Airlines had briefed their staff and organised transport.

As it was suspected that ISIS had somehow infiltrated the cabin crew of one of the major airlines, there was no choice but to vet all flight crew, cabin as well as cockpit. As the crew left the airplanes landing at Indira Gandhi airport in Delhi, they were all, without exceptions, escorted under armed guard to waiting busses.

The drive to the High Commission was tedious and on arrival, there were three busses waiting outside with tired and irritable occupants. Inside there were nearly sixty crew waiting to be processed. It was chaotic, deliberately so. The crew were required to produce their passport, photos were compared and then the passport was retained while security checks were run.

David Foal sat in the small office with the pile of passports in front of him in boxes. The door opened and another box of twenty of so passports were placed on the desk by his female assistant. "What exactly do these security checks involve?" she asked.

"They, sort of, involve me sitting here looking at these boxes of passports, for about another twenty or thirty minutes, until I have about a hundred. "

"Then what?" she asked.

Then I shall sort them by sex and hair colour and approximate age and height."

"Whatever for?"

"All will become clear,"

Some forty minutes later, the airline crews were all gathered together in the reception hall. Nearly one hundred and sixty had been rounded up in total. Foal addressed them, "Ok listen, we have now run our checks. When your name is called, please come forward to collect your passport and join the queue to board your bus to return to the airport. From the airport, you will join you flight or be transported back to your hotel accommodation, for those not on duty." Their was considerable moaning from those who were tired after long haul flights and were eager to get to their hotels.

The names began to be called, twenty men followed by twenty or thirty women. They were trooped out and loaded on the waiting busses. "Tina Westlake," Foal called.

She stepped forward, dressed in a British Airways uniform and pulling the standard overnight flight bag. Foal compared her picture and handed the passport back. "Off you go, good luck."

Charlotte Carter was no longer ginger. She liked the new blonde look the hairdresser had given her and she liked the uniform. The new passport in the name of Tina Westlake was genuine and had been suitably doctored as to visas and entry stamps to show she had travelled extensively as a stewardess.

The police stationed around the High Commission were confronted with bus after bus of uniformed airline staff and thanks to a bit of sorting by Foal, they were grouped into similar body types. Charlotte's bus left unhindered for the airport.

At the airport, she joined the rest of the crew and passed through security and passport control without challenge. She was just another member of the flight crew being transported back to be in the correct location for her next flight. Sitting in the jump seat, she was on her way back to Heathrow and England. Foal had organised the repatriation of Gil's coffin for her by a specialist carrier. She would collect it at the airport of her arrival.

"Fuck, fuck, fuck," said Delhi Police Chief, Reyansh Dutta as he put down the phone. He had just received a call from his informant, a local cleaner in the High Commission.

He checked the flights out of Indira Gandhi airport before making the call to the Chinese Embassy. "I am sorry, Charlotte Carter has managed to evade us and is on a flight to England."

Chapter 31

"The Commissioner has arrived," a voice announced over Tim's phone.

"Gather everybody in the conference room. I will join everyone in a few minutes<" said Tim in response.

This was it then thought Tim. It was only a matter of time before the can of worms was opened and he was, potentially, facing a murder charge. Did he regret the deaths of the three Russian scumbags that had been responsible for so many deaths, including his wife's? They could rot in hell as far as he was concerned.

Would he do the same again? He would. His only regret was that they had quick deaths. He would have preferred to see them hung by their balls and die slowly in agony.

He stood up and rubbed his eyes. He made his way to the window and gazed out onto the cold January morning air. He had a clear view of the comings and goings below. It was a good view, a very good view. It was a view he suspected he would not have for very much longer. The next view, he guessed, would be of the cell walls of one of Her Majesty's Prisons.

Tim left his office and passing the array of assistants and advisors clustered on his floor, made his way to the conference room. He approached the door and took a deep breath before pushing the double doors open. A step into the unknown perhaps? They were seated and waiting.

"Good morning all," he said cheerily. His happy demeanour took the assembled by surprise. Denham had taken the seat at the head of the table. The seat usually occupied by the Head of MI5, Tim's seat. On one side sat Christopher Moon, newly appointed Commissioner of Police and Denham's old chum. Two other police types were seated to Moon's left.

Tim stood staring at them for a moment and then focused on Denham, his second in command. "You seem to be jumping the gun a bit Harry. Now there's a good chap and get the fuck out of my seat." Tim was not going to be put on the back foot. He was not going to roll over and play dead. Denham was a talentless, petty minded, pen pusher who was jealous at Tim's rapid ascent to power at the agency.

Denham's face turned red and he was furious at the loss of face and Tim's put down. Almost shaking with rage, he rose to his feet and like a petulant child moving position.

"Now gentleman, what is this all about?" said Tim.

"You know very well what this is about," said Denham.

"Please be quite for a moment and allow our esteemed Police Commissioner to tell us."

Christopher Moon had not expected such a robust response from Tim and was slightly wrong footed. Denham had given the impression that, confronted with the file and evidence, Tim would have had to admit his complicity in the death of the Russians.

"I sent you a file that came into our possession from an undisclosed source,"

"Please do not treat me like a fool," said Tim. "You know and I know that good old Harry here has been feeding you information. This information is classified and after these accusations are proved baseless I shall ensure that Mr Denham will be facing charges of his own for breaching National Security."

"Irrespective of how the information came into my possession, I am investigating the possible murder of three foreign nationals on British soil. On the face of it, the information in my possession shows that a phone call was made from this building to a chauffeured car rental company. Subsequent to that call, the car minus driver was delivered to someone. The car was then used in the deaths of the three victims."

"An explanation has already been provided in that the Russians were leaving that day and MI5 had no further interest in them," said Tim.

"We were forced to accept that explanation given initially because we had no access to the computerised log that tracks and monitors all calls at MI5. Now we have the new evidence supplied to us, we have been granted permission by the Home Secretary to examine the call logs forensically." He placed the order signed by the Home Secretary on the table.

Tim picked up the single sheet of paper and read.

"As you see," continued Moon. "It orders you to recluse yourself from any involvement in the investigation."

Denham could not resist pitching in. "Do you know why you have been sidelined?" he smirked, "because you made that phone call."

"You are entitled to your opinion, Harry, but like so many of your opinions it will prove to be worthless," responded Tim.

"These two officers will be making the investigation. I introduce Superintendent Evesham, who has many years of experience in investigating complex cases and our head of Computer Forensics, Superintendent Low." The two nodded. "They, of course, have unlimited access to all the resources available to Scotland Yard."

Tim got the message. Moon was throwing everything the Met had at its disposal at him. Denham's chum was out to nail him whatever the cost.

"Should you attempt at any stage to interfere in the investigation, either directly or indirectly, you will be arrested and charged," said

Moon.

Tim rose from his seat. "You may turn out to be the shortest serving Commissioner the Met has ever had," he said as he left the room.

"How did it go?" asked Harriet as he entered his office where she had been waiting to talk to him.

"I am fucked," was he simple response.

"I think you are being overly pessimistic."

"No, just realistic, there is no way that that they will not trace that call back to me. There is no way of removing or altering those computer call logs."

"I know I played a large part as Head of Cyber Security here in ensuring that. I am proud of my work. They are unalterable even by me," said Harriet. "Sorry."

"It is what it is. Why are you here?"

"Charlotte Carter," said Harriet.

"Bugger! I am getting distracted. How did it go?"

"Brilliantly, she is on a plane to Heathrow as we speak. We got her out of the embassy in the confusion caused with the MI6 terrorist alert, without causing an International incident with the Indians. You set up that fake alert with Bernard Waverly at MI6. Didn't you?"

"A bit naughty, but all's well that ends well," said Tim.

"What now?" said Harriet?

"You go and collect Charlotte from the airport and hopefully, the formula for the new lightweight armour. I have an appointment with the Parliamentary under Secretary of State, John Maitland, at the Department of Science Laboratory. Hopefully now that Reese Williams is no longer fuelling the unrest at the Ban Dan Steelworks, we can sort the whole thing out."

"Charlotte is collecting Gil's coffin at the airport. So I shall accompany her and attend to that first before bringing her here."

"Right," said Tim, "we will all meet back here in a few hours".

Chapter 32

Tim had not expected the mob of civil servants at the meeting with Department for Business, Energy & Industrial Strategy and The Defence Science and Technology Laboratory. It was like a barn dance for old Etonion and Oxbridge alumni. Tim was not in the habit of wearing his old school tie, but with this job lot, he felt he should just not to stand out.

The two directors from the Ban Dan Corporation fitted right in. Their family's wealth had assured them of the "right" education. They were reuniting with old school and universities chums, left, right and centre. The Home Secretary was there along with a clutch of junior ministers. Tim spotted Maitland and one or two others he recognised.

They settled around the large oval table. The Home Secretary, with his advisors sat behind him, occupied one side, flanked by the two Departmental heads from the DSTL and Business.

"I am here to make the opening remarks and then I shall leave you to thrash out the details," said the Home Secretary. "Her Majesty's Government recognises the strategic importance of steel to the UK, not only in terms of independence of production but also as a major employer in Wales. As you are all aware, following the Countries Referendum decision to exit the European Union, we actively encourage the manufacturing industry to continue to stay and export. You are doubtless aware that we have obtained commitment to this effect from a number of Japanese car makers. Today we are hopeful that an accommodation can be worked out to ensure that our Indian partners at Ban Dan Steel continue their operations at Port Talbot. I shall leave you all to the detail, but rest assured, we are fully committed to maintaining steel production within the United Kingdom and will do all in our power to support you in your endeavours. I thank you."

Having clearly stated that the Government were open to doing a sweetheart deal with Ban Dan, the Minister left and the floor was taken by a representative from the Department for Business, Energy & Industrial Strategy. "I am here to talk about the Department for Business, Energy & Industrial Strategy's Accelerator funds. We fund innovative research that could be of advantage for the UK armed forces and national security. From our discussions with The Defence Science and Technology Laboratory, who have been investing in a new industrial process, that there may be significant, funding available to The Ban Dan Corporation to further the project."

Maitland, who had assumed the Chair of the meeting, introduced Tim. He rose to his feet. "I represent the Secret Service and should like to make The Directors of the Ban Dan Company aware, that we have been working with the Defence Science and Technology Laboratory in securing, for the UK Government, the details of a process for the manufacture of new, lightweight and cost effective armour. The new armour is less bulky and not composite in nature but steel based. I am not a metallurgist and refer in broad terms to the form of the armour to give you a flavour of its innovative nature and potential financial viability. More to the point, I am here to tell you that MI5 have the full details of the production process in their possession. I can also confirm that I have been authorised, that if a satisfactory deal is struck between the Government and Ban Dan, to release the full details to Ban Dan."

Tim had hoped that MI5 would have had Dr Huang's process actually in his possession before making the statement. It was only a matter of a few hours before Charlotte landed and Harriet returned with her and Gil's phone containing the formula.

The Director heading the Ban Dan Company's negotiating team rose to his feet. "We should first like to say that we are overwhelmed by the kind interest that the UK Government is showing in our small family run business. We, as you know, have a number of UK manufacturing based businesses, most notably, apart from Ban Dan Steel, are the Ban Dan car manufacturing plants. As you know, we produce, market and export a number of the most prominent British brands in the luxury market."

There was a deliberate pause while he allowed the significance of the statement to sink in to the assembled. The message was loud and clear. Yes, Ban Dan would continue to pump money into the ailing Steelworks in Port Talbot and they would take it from the Government to ensure that the jobs were preserved, but the sting in the tail was, they too wanted the kind of incentives offered to the Japanese to ensure that their cars remained competitively priced in the export market.

He continued his address. "Since we last examined the situation at Port Talbot there have been a number of favourable key changes that have minded us to revise our decision to discontinue production or sale the operation. Firstly, there has been an almost twelve percent devaluation in the value of sterling. This has had two major results. One, the cost of our steel to foreign buyers has dropped in real terms. Two and much more significantly, the pension shortfall has been reduced by almost sixty percent. The majority of the pension funds investments were invested in overseas assets and these have naturally appreciated in value, in line with the fall in sterling. To add to this turn around, the worker unrest at the plant has come to an end and talks are making progress and are wholly positive."

"We should therefore like to announce our continued commitment to steel production in the UK. We will also be more than pleased to take on the production of the new light weight armour with the support of the Department for Business, Energy & Industrial Strategy and The Defence Science and Technology Laboratory. There is, of course, much detailed work to be gone through before pen can be put to paper. We do feel that the Government and Ban Dan should make a joint statement to the press."

Maitland approached Tim as he gathered up his bits and pieces and began putting them in his Briefcase. "Thank you for help in retrieving our lost formula and making this possible."

"Always glad to be of assistance," said Tim.

"That is, if I still have a job," he said as he made his way back to Thames House.

Chapter 33

The Boeing 787-9 taxied down the runway and was cleared for takeoff. Charlotte sat in the jump seat and looked back down the length of the cabin as the aircraft accelerated and took off. She was on her way back to England.

Her seat on her return trip was a mile away from the luxury she and Gil had enjoyed on their outward journey. They had been in first class where there were just eight seats in the compartment. It had been champagne all the way. Now, sat on the small flip down seat in economy, she felt his absence.

The High Commission had taken care of all the arrangements to repatriate Gil's body. It was hard for her to come to terms that he was in a coffin, in the hold of a cargo plane, heading for Heathrow. The coffin would land and be disembarked two hours before she herself arrived at the airport.

The High Commission had been helpful organising everything. Normally the level of assistance she was afforded would not have been available to others in her situation, but given she could not have left the Commission without being arrested by Dutta, they were more than happy to step in. It, of course, did no harm that she had Dr Huang's process in her possession, stored on Gil's mobile. It also helped that Gil had left her a very rich woman.

She was finding it hard to manage her feelings. The joy on Gil's face on hearing he was to be a father replayed over and over in her mind as she drifted into sleep. Then the horror of his stabbing replaced the scene. The blood and the ambulance ride, a jolt as the plane hit turbulence jolted her awake. In her dream it was a bump in the road and the ambulance shaking that roused her. Confused she looked around.

She retrieved the paperwork and looked at the arrangements to recover Gil's body. She would need to make her way to the cargo area, where she needed to identify herself to customs. The coffin should, by the time she arrived, have been cleared for entry into the Country. She needed to present her true passport and not the new one provided by David Foal, when she departed on the bus, with all the other airline crew.

She studied the pile of paper work Foal had handed her before she left the High Commission. Tollman and Sons were the funeral directors that the freight carrier, who were flying Gil back, normally used to collect the deceased from the airport. They would deal with all the customs formalities for her. They were based in Staines, a town close to the airport. Collecting coffins from Heathrow being repatriated from around the World had become a significant part of their business. Partnering with the Freight Company that actually transported the coffins had benefited both parties.

It seemed so hard to think that in a few hours she would have to turn up and collect her lover's body. She felt as though it would be like responding to an undelivered parcel, where a card had been put through the letter box by the postman at your house. Name, ID, sign, "here's you parcel, madam". The tears came into her eyes as she thought of Gil, all alone in his box. She became aware that a number of her fellow passengers were gazing at her curiously. She quickly turned her head away and wiped her tears. It was not a good idea to attract attention.

She focussed back on the papers on her lap, trying to put the image of Gil from her mind. Foal had explained in detail what would happen at Heathrow airport after she had cleared immigration and customs. She had not really paid attention.

She found the hand written note he had prepared on realising that what he was saying was not sinking in. She would be met by someone from the UK Secret Service. She would be accompanied to retrieve Gil's body and after she had satisfied herself that she was happy with the arrangements, that Tollman and Sons had put in place, she would be taken to a safe MI5 house for debriefing.

She read the name of the MI5 contact that would escort after she landed, Harriet Shaw. As Charlotte exited the customs area she merely had to look for her name written on a piece of white card, held up by Harriet.

****

Tim arrived back from his meeting with Department for Business, Energy & Industrial Strategy and The Defence Science and Technology Laboratory to find Harriet in his office. "How did it go?" she asked as he sat.

"Well for now we're the heroes. Ban Dan will carry on making steel in the UK, jobs are guaranteed, pensions sorted and they will make the new light weight armour using Dr Huang's process that we will be giving to them."

"Except, we don't actually have the formula for the armour," said Harriet.

There is that small detail," said Tim.

"And," said Harriet, "Denham will probably have you clapped in irons in the next few hours."

"I must admit the whole situation is less than perfect. There is no avoiding what Christopher Moon, the Met Commissioner and his colleagues find. It is what it is and there is nothing I can do about that. We can, however, ensure that we recover the missing formula to ensure that Britain takes the lead in the production of the new lightweight armour. The last thing we need is The Changpu Corporation and the Chinese getting their hands on it. They may not have picked up the Ban Dan Steel Works in Port Talbot for a song, but it will not take them too long before they can commission their own production facility. We need that formula."

"I have been in touch with David Foal at the High Commission in Delhi. He is on our payroll, doing the job you used to do in Paris, gathering information for the Ambassador. I am meeting Charlotte Carter when she gets off the plane. I shall help her deal with the collection of Gilroy Jones's body, then take her to a safe house and debrief her."

"Not really your job," said Tim.

"I know, but given the situation with you under investigation, I think the only card you may have to play, before you are stitched up by Denham and Moon, is Huang's formula."

"You are so kind to me," said Tim.

"It is not all altruism, you know that."

"Silly me," said Tim. "Would it to be more the fact that your cart is hitched to my horse?"

"Well you did let me off the hook for spying on you for Elaine, our sadly deceased and disgraced boss."

"Ah! Yes now that you mention it, she was sort of guilty of treason or something. Wasn't she?"

****

Harriet paid the taxi and walked into arrivals at Heathrow. She looked up at the flight indicator board and was pleased to see that the British Airways Flight was on time and had landed. She made her way to the arrivals gate.

She had no intention of holding up a sign with Charlotte Carter written on it, advertising her arrival to all and sundry. She opened up the gallery on her phone and brought up Charlotte's passport photograph.

It was a photo of a young woman, approximately her own age, with bright red hair. "Well, she should be easy to pick out," Harriet thought, as she watched the various flight crews exit. Stewardess after stewardess came out dressed in the BA livery. There was one red head but she was too old. Harriet was confused. She looked more closely at the photo on her phone.

There remained one female cabin staff standing casually looking at the various people lined up holding signs with names on. She was a blonde. Harriet looked closely at the features and approached her." Miss Carter?" she said.

"Miss Shaw," responded Charlotte hesitatingly.

Chapter 34

Terrence Mailer woke earlier on the last day of his visit to China. Tomorrow, he, his aids, advisors and the whole circus would continue on to the Philippines and Japan. Although new to the job, he felt things were going well. His predecessor had laid the groundwork when he visited a year ago. A lot had changed since then in the UK. A new Prime Minister and the referendum that would see the UK leave the European Union.

His job had been to expand on the previous Foreign Secretary's success. This was an opportunity to firm up and expand the UK's deepening cooperation with the Chinese. He had a packed schedule on his last day. There was the meeting with the Chinese Foreign Minister, Wang Yi. Mailer sat down to read his brief. The issues were wide ranging. China was a permanent member of the UN Security Council and establishing broad agreement over security issues was important. The situations in Syria, Afghanistan and Iran were areas he was hoping to expand on common ground. The threat posed by Islamic State and terrorism were a further key area the UK was looking for support.

The two areas that were the elephant in the room for all foreign diplomats visiting China was, as always, its continued support for North Korea and China's own human rights abuses. There was always a diplomatic dance with the Chinese over these matters.

The Chinese would truck no interference in their internal affairs and it was evident that their human rights record was appalling and would continue to be so. On the other hand, the Foreign Secretary needed to be seen to have raised the matter and that the UK Government was a strong critic of the Chinese in this area. This was key to any political party's success back home in the UK. The Government, any

Government, needed to be seen pro-democracy and anti oppression. On the other hand no Government wanted to actually offend one of the biggest trading economies in the World, especially with Brexit looming on the horizon.

North Korea was for Mailer and the UK Government a rock and a hard place. It was clear to any rational individual that the Country was run by one of the worst dictators on the planet. It was also certain that they were developing a nuclear capability. China, on the other hand, had been key in the Country's formation when it had intervened militarily against the UN and the predominantly US and UK troops in nineteen fifty. Hostilities ceased in nineteen fifty three and the Peninsular was divided between North and South Korea at the thirty eighth parallel. China's support for the rogue state, however, seemed to be unshakeable.

Mailer's staff were engaged in a to and fro exercise with their Chinese opposite numbers to come up with a form of words that would allow the Foreign Secretary and the Chinese Foreign Minister to make a joint press statement. This would imply that significant progress had been made over North Korea, Chinese Human rights and that it was subject to ongoing dialogue. Everyone could claim success and nothing would change.

"How is my press statement coming along," asked Mailer.

"As to be expected," replied the aide. "We are nearly there. Your meeting with the Justice Minister implies some sort of progress on Human rights in China."

"It does?" joked Mailer. "That man's concept of the law is on a par with Judge Jeffries and the Witch Finder General. The judge was known as the 'Hanging Judge' and the other a puritan fanatic who liked burning people at the stake. Neither was renowned for their enlightened views.

"I think we can imply some sort of softening of the Chinese attitude on North Korea, though,"

"Are you sure?"

"They seem to be willing to partake in some form of statement condemning Kim Jong-un and the latest round of nuclear missile testing."

"That is something I suppose," said Mailer.

"More to the point, we are making progress on trade, real progress. Further, we are getting commitment to their money being invested in the UK. Let's face it, that is why we are here, money, not human rights."

"Just don't tell anyone?" said Mailer.

They were interrupted by the delegation's 'roady'.

"Are we together on the move to Manila?"

"All packed up and ready to roll. Finish your dinner with the Premier, a goods night sleep and then off to the airport early tomorrow. Next stop the Philippines."

Mailers day went well and the World's and, in particular, the UK press seemed to view the joint communiqués he issued with the Chinese Foreign Minister, the Minister of Justice and the Premier favourably. He went to bed a happy man and even enjoyed the food at the banquet.

Next morning, the logistic nightmare began. A mountain of luggage and paperwork had to be transported to the airport. Sensitive information needed to be tracked and guarded scrupulously and kept away from prying Chinese Intelligence. Every piece of electrical equipment, from phones to laptops needed to be checked for bugs and mal-ware. The delegation was accompanied by a small army of computer wiz kids who had been in a constant battle in cyber space with the Chinese hackers during the course of the visit. Then there were the translators, medical staff, and the host of civil servant and advisors, all of whom had to be boarded on the waiting plane. The journalist that accompanied the road show had to be briefed and moved to the airport.

Finally, and not smoothly, the plane sat on the runway at Beijing airport, waiting for the Foreign Secretary to step on board. There was a bit more hand shaking, red carpet treading and band playing before the cabin doors were closed and the plane set off for Manila.

"What a bloody palaver," said Mailer. "I have never shaken so many hands and nodded my head so often. There must have been a hundred of them rolled out to say goodbye."

"There are quite a few Chinese in the World," commented his aide. Miler smiled.

Ling Ling was overwhelmed by the experience of flying for the first time. Crammed in the economy section with the rest of the rank and file she looked from the window. She was confused and disorientated. A day ago she was a poor student in Beijing, now she was on a jumbo jet travelling the Globe. She was out of China and out of the control of the State. She did not understand what was happening, but she was excited by her new freedom. She had a British passport in her handbag and a ticket from Manila to London, England.

Chapter 35

Superintendents Evesham and Low sat in one of the interview rooms in Thames House. Knowing what they were looking for and the exact date and time had made life easy for the computer forensics team at Scotland Yard. They knew when the call, cancelling the Chauffeur to collect the three Russians, who were subsequently assassinated, was made. In essence, all they were doing was tracking down who had made that call.

Kevin Drew entered the room and was asked to sit. His red hair was uncombed and he looked as untidy as he had on the night of Harriet's birthday. He had tried, on a number of occasions, to speak to her subsequently. She had more or less blanked him. Kevin had never had a proper girlfriend and he could hardly believe that he, of all people, had managed to pull one of the most vivacious and beautiful girls in the building. He had wanted more. It was clear that she did not. For her, and he now had accepted it, it had been a one off.

He took up his position opposite Evesham and Low. "We are videoing the interview, so that you are aware. Please state your full name for the record," said Low.

Drew gave his name. Evesham spoke. "Would you please give us a rough outline of your roll at MI5, who you report to and a rough idea of your daily routine?"

"Well, I am a senior analyst in the cyber intelligence division here at MI5.On a day to day basis I liaise with other agencies, including GCHQ and the National Cyber Unit among others, to asses threats and attacks targeted at the Security Services. "

"Who is your boss?"

"Ultimately it is Harriet Shaw but on a day to day basis I work for Mr Denham, Deputy Head of MI5."

"I understand you attended Miss Shaw's birthday celebrations last week. Is that the case?"

Drew was surprised by the line of questioning. "I am not sure what that has to do with the phone call made by Mr Burr."

"Let me stop you there. You just said the phone call made by Mr Burr, the head of MI5. How do you know this to be a fact? Have you inspected Mr Burr's log? If you have, that would suggest that you would be guilty of spying on the head of MI5."

"No, of course I haven't, I just assumed, well heard, that this was what this was about."

"You are concerning me Mr Drew. Which is it, assumed or heard?" said Low.

"I don't know."

"Who told you that Mr Burr had made this alleged phone call?"

"It is common knowledge, I suppose," said Drew.

"I see. Did Mr Denham tell you that he suspected that Mr Burr was implicated?"

"No, I have had no conversations with Mr Denham on the subject."

"So who told you about it?" Low continued.

"No one," said Drew.

"Then I ask you again, have you accessed Mr Burr's confidential security log?"

"I have already told you, no."

There was a pause and Drew felt the intensity of the questioning in the silence more than when the interrogation was in flow. His brain could not make sense of the hostility facing him. He racked his brain in an effort to make sense of it. What had he done?

"Mr Drew, returning to the evening of Miss Shaw's birthday, please give, us your account of what occurred?" said Evesham.

"I left work and met up with a number of colleagues in the Coal Hole pub on the Strand. Harriet was there and Mr Burr turned up and joined the celebrations for a brief period."

"What happened then?"

"A few of us continued to a club come restaurant in Covent garden."

"Who do you recall was present?"

"As far, as I can recall, Harriet, Wendy, Christine, Mary and George."

"Then what happened?" asked Low.

"We had some food and a few more drinks, listened to a band and went home."

"Are you sure?"

"Yes," replied Drew.

"Did you go straight home?" asked Evesham.

"Yes,"

"Did you go to Thames House after you left the Club?"

"No of course not," Drew was becoming flustered.

"Did you go to the Strand Palace Hotel?"

Drew realised he had been caught in a lie. He had thought to keep his night with Harriet to himself. He had assumed that she would not have mentioned it so he had played the gentleman. "Well yes ..."

157

"Please tell us the truth Mr Drew," said Evesham.

Drew hesitated and then committed to the telling the events of the evening. "Harriet and I seem to make a connection at the Club. We found ourselves on our own and shared a kiss. We decided to leave and went to the hotel."

"And then?" asked Low.

"Well, we had sex."

There was silence as Low and Evesham waited for him to continue. He said nothing. Evesham sighed, a sigh of irritation. "Did you spend the entire night together?"

"Yes," Drew was feeling hostility towards the two policemen and was now reluctant to answer.

"I ask you again. Did you at any stage leave your room at the hotel during the course of the night following your arrival with Miss Shaw and your subsequent departure in the morning?"

"Of course not," he replied.

"Mr Drew you have lied to us once, please do not compound the matter. I ask you one more time. Did you at any stage leave the hotel room? Pease think carefully before you answer."

"No, I did not."

"Evesham nodded to Low who spoke. "Mr Drew, I am arresting you on suspicion of trying to pervert the course of justice and warn you that further charges may be laid under the Counter Terrorism legislation. You do not have to say anything. But it may harm your defence if you do not mention, when questioned, something that you later rely on in court. Anything you do say may be given in evidence."

"Now Mr Drew, we shall continue the questioning under caution. Would you like a solicitor present?"

Chapter 36

"That is all the paper work complete. My colleague will release the deceased. The funeral directors will be out front in a few minutes, the car park is just two hundred metres to the right as you exit the Customs Offices. I just wish to say, my condolences on your loss Miss Carter." The Border Control Officer handed Charlotte back her copies of the paperwork.

"Are you alright?" said Harriet. Charlotte looked pale and fragile. Collecting Gil's body had proved more traumatic than she had envisaged. She thought she had prepared herself for this moment on the flight back from India. The truth was that there is nothing that can prepare you to collect the body of the person you love and the Father of your unborn child.

"I don't feel right somehow. This does not feel like it is real. I feel like I am on the outside looking at myself. I am not me. Why have I got blonde hair and dressed in fancy dress? Gil won't even know me like this." Tears began to form in her eyes and she began to shake. She was still wearing the British Airways uniform that she had been given to merge with the rest of the airline crew as they left the High Commission in Delhi.

Harriet addressed the Customs Official," Do you have a toilet?" He pointed out the Ladies sign.

"Listen," said Harriet. "Charlotte, take your bag, go to the toilets, wash your face and get into your own clothes. I shall go out and tell the Funeral Directors, that you will be a few minutes."

"You're right. I need to be myself. I need to be the person that Gil knew. I sound crazy don't I? He won't know will he? He'll never see me again." She was weeping fully, now.

"Don't be silly. You don't sound crazy. You just need to deal with this in your own way." Harriet put her arms around Charlotte and gave her a big squeeze. "Come on. Get changed. Wash your face. Put some make up on. You will be ready to get Gil." Charlotte made her way to the Ladies, pulling her flight bag behind her. Harriet made her way to the buildings exit and made her way to the waiting hearse.

She left the building and adjusted her eyes to the bright sunlight. The January day had been overcast and gloomy up to this point. Now the Sun appeared as she looked around for the hearse. She spotted it and made her way in the direction of the car and the waiting group surrounding it. On seeing Harriet approaching, the three men, dressed in black suits, straightened themselves and stood upright.

Harriet walked across the car park and approached the group. "My name is …."

She did not have time to finish her sentence. "Get in the car," said the Chinese looking man, dressed in the formal, black suit. She went to open her mouth. "Shut the fuck up," he continued and levelled a gun at her face.

****

That morning at Tollman and Son's Funeral directors, Mr Tollman senior, had an early appointment. He lived above the business with his wife and his youngest son. His eldest son had arrived for work and was sat with his Mother and younger sibling having breakfast in the kitchen when a bell rang indicating that there was an arrival in the Funeral parlour downstairs.

Mr Tollman emerged from the lounge and made his way past the kitchen to the downstairs. "I'll go, it must be that Mr Smith that called yesterday, late."

The two sons and their Mother continued to eat. Mrs Tollman got up and went to the kettle to top up the tea pot. The boys were eating their cooked breakfast of egg and bacon. It was a ritual they shared each morning. They had breakfast together as a family. There was a loud crash as the teapot fell, and smashed on the, tiled kitchen floor. The two men looked up from their food to see their Mother staring, open mouthed at the kitchen door. The men turned to follow their Mother's gaze. Standing in the doorway was a Chinese man pointing a gun. "Sit quietly," was all, he said.

The sound of footsteps could be heard coming up the stairs. Mr Toolman passed the kitchen door followed by two further men and went into the lounge. "Bring them in here."

The man with the gun gestured for the occupants of the kitchen to go into the lounge. When they entered the room, they found Mr Toolman sat at the desk in the corner. The lounge doubled as an office. The desk had a printer and a computer on it and a small filing cabinet next to it.

They sat in a line on the sofa watching as he went through the desk and produced some paper work. "Here it is." The man stepped forward and examined it. Satisfied, he stepped behind Mr Tollman. A knife seemed to appear in his hand from nowhere and in one expert action he cut his throat. Mr Tollman made one gasp as the blood pumped and he died. His two sons were transfixed, shocked watching the brutal killing of their Father.

The killing of Mr Toolman was the signal for the other two men to act. They stepped forward in unison and killed the two sons as their Mother watched. It was so fast that she could not get her brain to focus. Her husband and her two sons died and she had not even moved. The man who had slaughtered her husband took two steps and his knife found her heart. It had happened in a matter of seconds.

One by one the bodies were gathered up and taken to the funeral parlour downstairs and out to the preparation area. There were three coffins. They men placed thehusband and wife in one each and their two sons shared the other. They took the three black morning suits, from the hanger where they were stored, along with the white shirts and black ties.

Dressed, now as funeral directors, the three men sat in the hearse and headed for the airport. Chief Dutta, of the Delhi police, had been invaluable. He may have let Charlotte slip through his fingers in India, but had made good by letting the Changpu Corporation know when and where she would be arriving in the UK to collect Gil's body. The killers had the paper work, from Tollman and Son's, to recover Gil's body from customs.

****

Du Longwei drove the hearse at a steady pace as he left from the airport and turned onto the M4 motorway. It had all gone to plan. It had been easy. He had a description from Dutta of Charlotte Carter. She had been easy to identify with her bright red hair as she approached the customs area accompanied by the blonde British Airways stewardess. He thought that her companion might have presented a problem but, fortunately, she had not emerged with her.

"Now Miss Carter," Du Longwei said. "If you behave yourself, give me Mr Jones phone with Dr Huang's formula on it, and Mr Jones's password to unlock the phone, I might just let you live."

Harriet Shaw looked at Du Longwei, recognising him from his photo, driving from Port Talbot after meeting Reese Williams. She felt fear. She knew that he had killed at least two men, possibly more, without hesitation, Matthew Watling, the security Guard and John Tatum, both at Techmat Technologies. She realised that she was more than likely to be his next victim.

Chapter 37

Kevin Drew was completely confused by the turn of events. He sat opened mouthed, as the caution was read to him. "Do you want a solicitor present Mr Drew?" He was asked a second time.

"I don't understand." He said.

"Mr Drew, we would like to put a number of matters to you. Are you happy for us to proceed?" said Superintendent Low.

"What matters?"

"For the record, I am showing a transcript of the witness statement taken from Miss Harriet Shaw," said Evesham. He took the statement from the folder and placed it in front of Drew.

He began to read.

Question, "Would you please recount the events on the evening of your birthday?"

"We all met in the Coal Hole pub. There were a number of my workmates there during the course of the evening. At some time around ten or half ten, myself, Kevin along with Wendy, Christine, Mary and George went into Covent Garden for a meal."

Question, "What happened at the restaurant?"

"We were seated in a booth. We had more drinks and something to eat. There was a band playing. At some point the meal finished and we broke into smaller groups."

Question,"Then what occurred?"

"It all becomes a little vague after that. The last thing I remember is Kevin buying me a drink. I told him, I had enough, but he was very insistent, that I drank it. I didn't want to offend him."

Question," Do you have or did you have any romantic intentions towards Mr Drew?"

"Certainly not, he is and was just a work colleague."

Question, "And yet you left the Club and spent the night with him at the Strand Palace Hotel?"

"I remember none of that."

Question, "What is the next thing you remember?"

"Waking up in the morning in bed at the hotel with Kevin."

Question, "What did you do next?"

"I dressed and went home, changed and went to work."

Question, "You are in overall control of IT at Thames House aren't you?"

"Not in that sense, I do not run the computer system. I use the links, systems and develop algorithms to track and counter actual and potential cyber attacks. There are other analysts and programmers that actually maintain and upgrade the software."

Question, "Your security clearance, however, allows you access to all data and software, doesn't it."

"Yes, but as I said, that is not my role. I would have no need in the normal course of events to enter into the actual system. The only situation where I can envisage having to is if MI5 were being subjected to an all out Cyber attack by, say a hostile foreign government."

Question, "When was the last time that occurred?"

"Never, the system has never been breached."

Question, "How about on the night of your birthday?"

"I have already told you, I was with Mr Drew."

Question, "On a practical level, how would you gain access to the computer systems if you wanted to?"

"You would need my security id card with my micro chipped, encrypted information and my password."

Question, "So only you can access the computer security log, for example, the log that our Forensic Computer team are currently examining, in an attempt to track the source of a phone call made in connection with the murder of three Russian nationals."

"I have not accessed the log."

Question, "Where do you keep your id and passcode?"

"In my handbag, the code is stored on my mobile and my id is in my purse."

Evesham looked at Kevin Drew. "Do you agree with Miss Shaw's recollection of events the night of her birthday?"

"Yes, I would say that was more or less what happened."

"Did you at any stage during the course of the night leave the hotel room?" asked Low.

"No," replied Drew.

"I should like you to look at this video clip taken on the Hotel CCTV. It is time stamped three zero six." Low turned, the laptop computer he had in front of him round. Drew could see the screen as Low pressed play.

Drew watched what was, obviously, the view from a camera, situated in the corridor outside the bedroom at the Hotel. The door opened and he could be seen leaving the room and heading for the lifts. The footage had been edited together to then show him emerging from the lift into the foyer. The next clip was of the entrance doors where he could be seem leaving the building. "That's not me," he said.

Low laughed. "Who else is it leaving your hotel room, dressed in your clothes?"

Drew said, "I didn't leave the hotel."

Evesham pressed play. "Here is a video clip from the security camera here at Thames House.

The CCTV showed Drew entering the building and scanning his pass. The on duty Guard looked up from his newspaper and could be heard saying. "Working late?" There was no audible response. Drew appeared to keep his face from the camera, but his ginger hair was clearly visible from around the hood he had pulled up to keep the cold January night air out.

Drew sat mouth wide open as the video montage continued to play. He was seen to leave the building seventy minutes later. The next clip, just before five forty six, showed him re-enter the hotel room.

"I don't understand." Drew said.

"I think it is pretty obvious to anyone. You left the hotel, came here to Thames House, did something and returned to the hotel."

"I never left the room. Harriet confirmed that in her statement."

Evesham pressed play again. This clip showed Drew and Harriet arriving at the hotel. It was clear that Drew was, more or less, half dragging and half carrying her to the room.

"Miss Shaw seems to be in no condition to know if you stayed in the room or left. Does she?"

"I want a lawyer," said Drew.

"I am afraid that is not going to happen. We are upping the anti Mr Drew. We are going to charge you under the Anti Terrorism Legislation. In other words, in the interest of National Security, we are suspending your right to a lawyer so that there is no possibility of your detention becoming common knowledge. The added benefit is that there is no opportunity for you to communicate with any other party and foreworn them," said Low.

"Our Computer Forensic Team has provided us with one further piece of information that we should like you to comment on. While you were here at Thames House, the security phone call log was accessed using Miss Shaw's id."

"She was with me in the hotel," replied Drew.

"I think you had better reconsider your replies Mr Drew," said Low.

"We put it to you that the following sequence of events occurred that night. After the group of you left the pub and went to Covent Garden, at some stage, during your time at the Club, you administered some form of drug to Miss Shaw," said Evesham.

"Miss Shaw, in her statement, said you bought her a drink and were insistent that she drank it. What did you put in it, Rohypnor or GHB? They the easily available date rape drugs, are they not?" said Low.

"I didn't put anything in her drink."

"Having drugged Miss Shaw, you can bee seen dragging her to the hotel bedroom. Again, from her statement, we know that she remembers nothing further until she waked in the bed the following morning," said Low. He paused. There was no reply.

"While she was unconscious and inadvertently acting as your alibi, you made your way to Thames House and tampered with the call log."

"I did not access the computer system."

"No, you were smatter than that. You took Miss Shaw's id and used that. I am guessing that her phone was unlocked and you merely scrolled through and obtained her pass code from it."

"I didn't".

"You then accessed the call log in an attempt to hide the true identity of the caller, who was involved in the assassination of the three Russians. Did you not?"

"No,no," said Drew.

"Mr Drew, I suggest you come clean and tell us who you are working for."

Chapter 38

"Tell me what happened and give me as much detail as you can remember," said Tim.

Charlotte was in the interview room at Thames House. She had phoned the police when she emerged from the Customs shed and found the hearse and Harriet nowhere to be found.

"After presenting the paperwork to claim Gil's body, I decided I didn't want to be in fancy dress. I was still wearing the airline's uniform. I went to the toilet and changed my clothing. It just felt more appropriate."

"I understand."

"I came out expecting to see the hearse. At first, I did not know what to make of it, so I just waited. After about ten minutes, I went back inside and checked with the Customs Officer if there had been some sort of last minute problem. I thought they might have called the hearse and Miss Shaw back or something."

"Then what did you do?"

"I got the phone number of the undertakers, from their Invoice, which I printed off in the High Commission in Delhi. I then rang the number. There was no answer, so I went back outside and looked again. I was completely confused and did not know what to do."

"How long had it been now?"

"I am not sure, twenty minutes or half an hour. Then I phoned the police."

"How long did it take them to arrive?"

"About forty or fifty minutes, I think they thought it was a joke or hoax."

"So it was about an hour and a half after the hearse drove off that the police responded."

"Longer in actuality, they took ages to take down the details and report it, probably another twenty minutes."

"So it was nearly two hours before anyone was actually searching for the missing hearse," Charlotte nodded her head in agreement. Tim knew that the hearse in that time frame could be over a hundred miles away from the Airport.

"The police have still not managed to locate the hearse, but they have gained access to the Funeral Parlour. They discovered the bodies of Mr Tollman and his family, I am afraid," said Tim.

"Oh God," Charlotte was visibly shaken. "What is going on?"

""Don't worry. I am sure Gil will be found. The kidnappers wanted you. It is clear that they became confused with the hair colour and mistook Miss Shaw for you. I do, however, need your help in the meantime."

Charlotte took a deep breath. It was clear that she was deeply shocked by the recent events and finding it difficult to deal with them. "What can I do?"

"You have something that they want. I believe that you are in possession of the details of a process that Gil's friend, Dr Huang, was working on?

"It is on his phone. He gave it to me in the ambulance on the way to the hospital." She began to sob. It was clear, that she was close to breaking down as she recalled Gil's stabbing on the streets of Delhi.

"May I have it?" said Tim.

She reached inside her blouse and unhitched a body bag belt that she was wearing underneath, around her waist. She unzipped the belt and removed the phone. She handed it to Tim. The code to unlock the phone is, "charlotte 2807" It's my birthday. It was so he wouldn't forget it," she was crying now with the recollection.

"Thank you," said Tim. "You will be taken to a safe place and you will be assigned police protection until this is sorted out. Don't worry, we will find Gil and all this will be fine."

He waited with her until here escort arrived and watched as she left. He now had a bargaining chip, Gil's phone. He knew that it was only a matter of time before Harriet's abductors made contact for a trade. He started to leave the interview room when his mobile rang. He sat down and looked at the number. It was Harriet. It had not taken them long to realise they had the wrong red head.

"Anthony Burr," he answered. He knew that it would not be Harriet making the call. Her captors would not risk the chance that she might reveal her location.

"We have something you want, and you, I think by now, have something we want. Am I correct?" Tim was given full instructions in order to effect the trade of Huang's formula for Harriet Shaw's life.

He made his way back to his office. He found Harry Denham seated on a chair by the coffee table as he entered. "I assume you have the formula?" he asked, as Tim walked towards him.

"Yes, it was on Gil's phone."

"They have located the hearse with Gil's body in it by the way," said Denham.

"Good," said Tim.

There was long silence. Denham finally spoke again. "Give me the phone," he said.

"Fuck off," said Tim.

"You have to give the phone to Maitland at The Defence Science and Technology Laboratory."

"I don't have to do anything," said Tim.

"I know you intend to trade it for Harriet Shaw. I bet that her abductors have already made contact. Haven't they?"

"You forget who's in charge here. So I repeat, fuck off, Harry,"

"Well you won't be in charge for much longer. The Met will be charging you in the next twenty four hours. I have that from Christopher Moon, the Head of the Met. So I won't be the one fucking off, you will."

"Just get out of my office. I have stuff to do," said Tim.

"If you give the phone to the Chinese, you will be guilty of espionage. It is treason Tim. So stop digging a hole for yourself. You are in enough shit already."

"Get out."

"I can't do that. Now, will you hand it over or not?"

"Fuck off," repeated Tim.

Denham locked smug as he began to speak." I am formally arresting you on suspicion of intent to supply information to a Foreign Power. I am relieving you of your post immediately." He got up. "I am going to fetch security and have you detained. I have already spoken to the Home Secretary and have the authority. One last time, Tim, hand over the phone."

Tim raised himself to his feet as Denham stood over him, hand outstretched to receive Gil's phone. "I am sorry to do this," said Tim as he punched Denham square on the chin. He caught the unconscious man and lowered him to the floor. "I knew all that martial arts training would come in useful," he said as he laid Denham in the recovery position.

It was only the second time Tim had thrown a punch in anger. The other time was when he had stepped in to protect the woman who became his wife. He had started martial arts at Cambridge, now, nearly twenty years ago. He had just kept it up as a means of staying fit. He had won a few competitions when he was younger but no longer competed.

He made his out way of Thames House, onto the Street and headed for China Town.

Chapter 39

Tim had forgotten all about the Chinese New Year's parade and celebrations being held in the centre of London. He looked at his watch, he would have to get a move on if he was to comply with Du Longwei's instructions. The traffic was at a standstill as thousands of Londoners had descended on Trafalgar Square, Shaftsbury Avenue and China Town to witness the celebrations.

He saw the ridiculousness of the situation as he started to peddle a "Boris" bike towards China Town. The bikes, named after the ex Mayor of London, Boris Johnson, were, parked all over the centre of the Capital. You took one, paid a small fee and peddled to your destination. You then parked the bike, ready for the next person to use. Tim felt the day was becoming surreal. So far he had a coffin hi-jacked, his assistant kidnapped, punched his deputy and was now riding a bike through a parade of dancing dragons and giant marionettes on floats.

The Dragon, one of a few he was currently try to pass was a magnificent beast. It was red, white and blue, enhanced with gold. A policeman warned him to get out of the way of the advancing parade of floats, dancers, acrobats and musicians. As he got closer to China Town, he abandoned the bike and took to jogging.

He finally arrived at the Flowering restaurant. He was expected and shown straight into Zhen Zhou's office. "Mr Bur, so good to see you again" he said. The banging of drums and cymbals from the celebrations taking place outside could clearly be heard. The odd firework exploded adding to the noise.

"Do you have what is required?"

"I do," said Tim and handed the phone to Zhen.

Tim became aware for the first time of the second Chinese in the room. "This gentleman is an IT expert, sent here to examine the phone. "

"That is not the agreement. I have no intention of releasing the mobile to anyone from the Changpu Corporation until I have Miss Shaw."

"Neither do I. He will only examine the phone and then give it back to me. I shall keep it until Miss Shaw is safely returned to you. I guarantee that they will not get possession until I am satisfied that all the conditions of the trade are fully complied with. My reputation is at stake and I could never suffer such a loss of face that would follow if I were not to act honourably in this matter."

Tim handed the phone over. The IT expert took it from him and nodded his head politely, as though he was receiving a gift. He examined the contents of the phone and satisfied that it contained Dr Huang's plans for the production of the new light weight armour, returned it to Zhen.

There was an exchange in Chinese between the two before the IT expert left the office. Zhen turned to Tim. "You are to go to the entrance to China Town and wait. Miss Shaw will be reunited with you. I will phone Mr Du Longwei and tell him that I have the phone and that will instigate her release."

The area surrounding the Chinese Arch at the entrance was a mass of people. Tim found himself part of the crowd watching the activities. The sun had gone down on the cold January evening. The rhythm from the gongs and drums spurred the dragon to dance vigorously, shaking its head from side to side, it wound around the onlookers. The men inside caused it to leap in the air and shimmy and shake. Tim searched the crowd for Harriet.

Acrobats occupied the centre of the space in front of the crowd. Their costumes gold, red, yellow and blue were a sight for all to enjoy. Gasps came from the gathered throng as they formed pyramids, towers and leapt high into the air. Dancers moved in a blaze of colour to the music. Bright flashes of light lit the sky as fireworks were exploded with loud bangs. It was deafening and bringing an expolsion of colour, sound and light. The year of the Rooster was truly starting with a bang.

Tim studied the crowd intently. He hoped that Harriet would be returned. He realised that he was dependent on Zhen, acting as broker and surety for the exchange. It was his only security. Zhen was only to release Gil's phone to The Changpu Corporation when and only when Harriet had been returned. Once he had Harriet, Tim was to call Zhen confirming the fact.

Finally, he spotted Du Longwei. He stood in full view opposite Tim, studying the crowd for any signs of an MI5 trap. He stood stock still, checking his surroundings. There was no sign of Harriet. Tim felt the butterflies in his stomach as his concern grew for her safety.

Time seemed to stand still as the two watched each other for any sign of betrayal. Where was Harriet? A group of three masked dancers blocked Tim's view of Du Longwei briefly. They wore elaborate costumes and hideously carved masks. Tim had seen these types of characters before in Chinese opera. He had been required to attend a performance on their touring company when he was working at the Paris embassy. While it had been colourful, it had also been the most excruciatingly boring two hours of his life. To his untrained ears the performance had sounded as though a hundred cats were being systematically castrated, causing them to wail as loudly as possible.

One of the male dancers removed the mask of the female. It was Harriet. They pushed her forward and she ran to Tim. She stumbled and nearly collided with an acrobat doing back flips. She carried on and reached Tim's arms. He pulled her close. She was safe.

On the opposite side of the circle of spectators, watching the entertainers, Du Longwei turned and began to walk away. The Dragon danced into his path as he tried to make his getaway. It began to circle him. Fire crackers exploded with flashes and loud bangs. The Dragon danced off.

Du Longwei lay dead. At first no one noticed. Then there was a scream, hardly audible above the cacophony of the celebrations. The dragon continued to dance away from the scene. One of the dancers came out from inside the dragon costume and was replaced by another. The dragon danced further into China Town.

The gunman moved through the crowd unnoticed. He entered the Flowering Lotus restaurant. "It is done, the cunt is dead," he said to Zhen. Zhen smiled. He was finally rid of the parasite that had been on his back for years. It was an auspicious start to the New Year.

Chapter 40

Back at Harriet's flat, Tim sat waiting while Harriet showered. Flattering as the fancy dress costume was, she decided that she would prefer to go to Thames house in her own clothes. She emerged from the bathroom after about half an hour. She had a bath towel wrapped around her and her hair was still dripping from the shower.

"Tell me," said Tim, "Do blondes or red heads have the most fun?"

"She laughed. "Well, I am natural blonde and my excursion to the red side has only been a recent experience. In that time, I have been kidnapped by a group of body snatching, homicidal maniacs and forced to dance alongside a dragon. So, on balance, I think being a blonde was more fun. When I was blonde, the worst thing ever to happen to me was having a puncture, with no spare tyre, on the M25."

It was Tim's turn, to laugh. "I can see that, I am guessing that you will not be giving up your IT job in favour of becoming a field agent any time soon?"

"More to the point, when we get back to HQ, will either of us have a job?"

"I think you should be fine, but I am not so sure about me. Having clobbered my second in command and wandered off with the phone, with the formula on it, I am guessing the Home Office may be a bit nervous about my continued tenure. Add to that, the fact that the phone call that paved the way for the assassination of the three Russian, responsible for my wife's death and you may well conclude they have a point."

"Well, we all have the odd flaw. Yours just happens to be random violence. It is, possibly, not such a bad trait for someone in the espionage line of work," said Harriet, as she began using the hairdryer.

He watched her as she sat on the floor, her legs tucked beneath her. She had placed a small, free standing mirror on the coffee table in which she observed herself as she brushed her hair into its familiar style. She saw him looking and stared at him. There was a moment of sexual tension. It was clear from her body language that she felt the attraction between them.

Tim looked away. It did not feel right. It was too soon after his wife's murder. He busied himself by standing up and walking to the window. He feigned interest in what was happening the street below. The moment passed.

"I should, as your boss, offer you some form of trauma counselling after your recent experience," he said, to change the atmosphere.

She switched the hairdryer off and finished brushing her hair. "It is alright to allow yourself to feel again."

There was a silence. Not an embarrassed silence, but a calm that flowed between them. It was a recognition of a bond between them. Part lust and part sexual, it held out for possible future growth. Now, it was merely recognition that there was more.

"I'll get dressed."

"Yes, I think that might be a really good idea," said Tim. Harriet left the room as Tim recovered his composure.

He picked up his phone and dialled. Denham answered. "I am sorry about biffing you," said Tim in opening.

Denham was not that easily mollified. "Fuck off," came the retort.

The silence hung briefly between them. "We have tracked your mobile phone's signal to Miss Shaw's residence. There is a car on the way. You will be arrested and brought back to Thames House. The

Home Secretary is on the way to here, along with the Met Police Commissioner. The two investigating officers, Evesham and Low will also be attending to report on their investigation into who made the phone call from here leading to the Russian's deaths."

"It's a fucking party, anybody else coming?"

"John Maitland from the Defence Science and Technology Laboratory, who I am speculating will be very disappointed that you have handed over Miss Carter's phone to the Chinese with Classified, Top Secret information on it."

"I see, not a party, more a lynching," said Tim.

"I am assuming you successfully rescued Miss Shaw at the expense of National Security?" said Denham.

"I should have hit you fucking harder," said Tim as he cut the connection.

Harriet emerged, dressed for the office. "I just spoke to Harry," said Tim.

"Judging by the expression on your face, I suspect that it could have gone better?"

"You could say that. He has run straight to the Home Secretary, telling him I traded Huang's formula to the Chinese for your release. He has also got his mate, Christopher Moon, the Commissioner, to come over to make my arrest personally. He is planning a double whammy as they say, treason and murder."

"Look on the bright side. You never really wanted the job anyway. You only took it to find your wife's murderers," said Harriet.

"You do have a point, but I would prefer not to spend the next thirty years banged up at Her Majesty's pleasure," replied Tim as they made their way to the door out of the flat.

They took the lift down to street level and stepped out onto the pavement. The two Special Branch officers immediately approached him. One spoke, "you are to come with us Sir, Will I need to use handcuffs?"

"No, that won't be necessary. Is it OK if Miss Shaw rides with us?" said Tim.

The Officer looked at his colleague for direction. The other spoke addressing Tim. "I don't see why not. We have no instructions to the contrary. If you get in the rear of the car with my colleague, she can ride upfront with me."

Chapter 41

"Well this is jolly," said Tim. The Home Secretary, Met Police Commissioner, the Parliamentary under Secretary of State, John Maitland from the Defence Science and Technology Laboratory, Harry Denham and Harriet Shaw were all seated with him at the conference table in Thames House. It had been a long day and it was nearly midnight as Denham took the floor.

"It is with deep regret that I find myself in this position," began Denham. "I find myself having no option, but to bring to your attention the serious charges facing Mr Burr, the head of MI5. The security of the Country has been placed at risk, owing to his actions. The Charges are serious and have widespread security implications at home and abroad." He paused and glanced at the papers on the table. He was savouring the moment of his triumph. He should have been given the job as head of MI5 and now was his time to gloat.

"I intend to deal with the latest incident first," he continued. "Earlier today, we came into possession of top secret information relating to the method of producing a new light weight armour. The process was developed at Techmat Technologies, in association with the Government's Defence Science and Technology Laboratory, by Dr Stanley Huang. A plot was foiled, by MI5, of an attempt by Chinese Company, The Changpu Corporation and the Chinese Government, to gain control of the Ban Dan Steel works. Their aim was to gain a monopoly on the manufacture of the armour by stealing the formula and using the steel works to manufacture it," he paused to allow the magnitude of the plot to sink in to the assembled.

"Mr Burr had possession of the formula for the manufacture of the new amour. However, regrettably, during the recovery of the formula, Miss Shaw, the head of MI5's Cyber Security section, was taken hostage by persons employed by the Chinese. Their intention was a trade, Miss Shaw for the formula."

The Home Secretary spoke. "As is widely known, it has been the Governments stated position that it will not trade with terrorists. It must be said that I assume that MI5 is fully aware of this. I fear that, seeing Miss Shaw present, glad that I am sure we all are, that she is fit and well, that such a trade has taken place?"

"Mr Burr handed the formula to the Chinese this afternoon to secure her release. I attempted to stop him and was physically assaulted during the process," said Denham. "I have no alternative to accuse Mr Burr of supplying top secret information to a foreign power," a smug smile of satisfaction spread across Denham's face as he resumed his seat.

Tim stood. There was total silence in the room as those present contemplated the scandal that was about to break on their heads, as the head of MI5 was to be arrested for espionage. "I feel that Mr Denham seems to be misdirecting himself as to the events of today. As I see matters, Mr Denham was seized by a fit of insanity in my office. He made a series of deductions and convinced himself that I was some sort of enemy agent. At no point did I inform Mr Denham that I was going to breach national security and hand over classified information to a foreign power."

Tim was interrupted by Denham." You can't deny it. The proof is in front of us all, unless that is a hologram, we can plainly see Miss Shaw is seated at the table."

"As I said, Mr Denham's imagination seems to be getting the better of him. May I be allowed to continue and to clear up this bit of nonsense?"

"Please continue," said the Home Secretary.

"I will not bore you with operational details but in brief, Miss Shaw was abducted by an agent by the name of Du Longwei. Mr Du Longwei is a suspect in a murder investigation being conducted by the Cambridgeshire Police. They believe he was used by The Changpu Corporation to stir up unrest at the Ban Dan steel works so they could buy the facility at a knock down price and to acquire the formula by murdering the CEO of Techmat. In any event, their investigation will be somewhat curtailed as Mr Du Longwei was murdered in China Town today."

"Who murdered him?" asked Moon.

"I don't know," said Tim." I suspect that the Triad gangs that operate in London may well have been involved. In any event murder, is a matter for the police to investigate."

"Sir John, could I ask you to get up and come over to me please?"

Maitland, slightly puzzled, made his way round the table to Tim.

"Here is the phone containing the formula, which Mr Denham accuses me of passing to the Chinese." He handed Gil's phone to the under Secretary. "Would you please confirm it contains the information to the rest of the people sat around the table?"

Maitland took a few minutes to look through the document stored on the mobile. "It is all here," he said, before returning to his seat.

"I apologise to Mr Denham for having to use physical force to stop in him interfering in my carrying out my lawful duties. I do now, however, expect Mr Denham to withdraw all his wild accusations against me." Said Tim as all eyes turned to Denham.

Denham was visibly shaken by the fact that Tim still had the phone in his possession. He composed himself. "I reserve my apology until the next charge is dealt with," he responded.

Chapter 42

The atmosphere in the conference was tense as Denham continued to speak. "There is another more serious charge against Mr Burr that needs to be addressed," Denham's voice gained confidence as he spoke. "I believe that Mr Burr conspired with ISIS backed terrorists to bring about the deaths of the three Russians while they were on British soil. A phone call was made from MI5, here at Thames House, that removed MI5 protection and surveillance from these Russians and allowed ISIS access to the car rented by MI5 to transport them. The car subsequently exploded, killing all three. The bomb was traced back to a known ISIS bomb maker." He paused to let, the gravity of the accusations be fully understood.

He sat and Moon rose. "I, at Mr Denham's request, instructed my officers to conduct a full investigation in order to identify the individual that placed that call." He walked to the door and returned a moment later with Superintendents Low and Evesham in tow. "Please gentleman, make you report."

"We have conducted an inquiry into the secure phone log maintained by MI5 that records all communications made," said Low. "I will ask Superintendent Evesham to read our findings to you."

Evesham cleared his throat and began to read. "One, we found that the call had been made from this building to the car rental company. Two, we cannot say with any level of certainty who made the call."

There was a look of astonishment that passed between Moon and Denham. Moon recovered himself first and spoke. "I want a full explanation and details now," he commanded.

"With respect Sir, we have not discussed the matter with Crown Prosecution Service and there could be very serious charges brought. We would not wish to compromise matters in the meantime," said Low.

"For God's sake, I am the Home Secretary. Spit it out, now."

"If you insist," said Evesham. "Our investigation revealed that, the day before our examination of the computer log was to commence, it was accessed and tampered with. The person who accessed the log was initially identified as Miss Shaw. Further investigations revealed that it was, in fact, a Mr Kevin Drew."

Denham rose to his feet. "What are you taking about, Kevin cannot gain access to that part of the system, his security clearance level would prohibit it. This is nonsense."

"Well, you would say that wouldn't you," retorted Evesham.

"What are you saying? Are you accusing me?"

"As I said, the matter is with the CPS and no one is accusing anyone at this juncture. Shall I continue?"

The Home Secretary spoke. "Please continue superintendent and Harry, shut up."

"As I was saying, initially we thought that an attempt had been made by Miss Shaw to change the log to cover up for her boss Mr Burr. On closer examination, we found that Mr Drew appears to have drugged Miss Shaw at her birthday celebration and taken her to nearby hotel. There, while she lay unconscious, he took her security id, made his way here, entered the building and gained access to the log. He then returned to the hotel where Miss Shaw was to have been his alibi. The whole plot came unravelled when we uncovered CCTV at the hotel and here at Thames House showing Mr Drew clearly leaving the hotel and entering this building," said Low as he sat.

Evesham took over. "I read a statement taken from Mr Drew. I should state that Mr Drew was effectively offered immunity from prosecution on the conditions that he made a complete and full admission of guilt. I believe that the CPS took that decision based on the importance of knowing the full details on national security grounds."

He began to read. "I Kevin Drew make the following statement freely and confirm that I have been informed of my legal right to remain silent and my right to have a solicitor in attendance "

"Please, just the jump to the relevant sections," said the Home Secretary.

"Shall I just summarise?" asked Low. The Home Secretary nodded.

"Please do."

"Well, he describes how they went to a club and he put GHB in Miss Shaw's drink. He then confirms he left her asleep at the hotel and borrowed her ID from her handbag. He then came here, accessed the computer and tampered with the log before returning to the hotel where Miss Shaw was still asleep."

"But who instructed him to do this?"

Evesham rose to his feet. "Mr Harry Denham, we are arresting you on a charge of attempting to pervert the course of justice."

Chapter 43

"What the fuck happened there?" said Tim as Denham was taken away to be cautioned.

Harriet thought back to her birthday bash that saw her and Drew end up alone.

Harriet had put a great deal of effort into seducing Drew. He lay on his front on the bed in the Strand Place. She had hooked up with him at her birthday meal in Covent Garden. She could not help feeling slightly revolted by his thin and spotty white body. She continued her prostrate massage with one hand and reached into her handbag, beside her on the bed, with the other.

Drew continued to groan in ecstasy as she slid her finger in and out of his rear. She found what she was looking for in her handbag. She withdrew the suppository. He felt nothing as she slid the pill up his back passage. The drug would quickly be absorbed through the lining of his rectum. It was a powerful sedative.

She realised that Drew's groans of pleasure were now snoring. She jumped from the bed and went to the bathroom and washed her hands. She returned to the clothing placed on the chair. She dressed, not in her blouse and skirt, but in Drew's clothing. She put his outer coat on and pulled the hood up that could be unfolded from the collar. With the collar up as well, only her eyes and a small amount of hair was visible.

She checked herself in the mirror. Her recently dyed red hair was an almost perfect match to Drew's ginger locks. He was a small individual and she, although slimmer and curvier, could easily pass as him. She went through his wallet and retrieved his security pass to Thames House.

She opened the door and left the bedroom. She knew he would not stir for hours. She, despite feigning drunkenness, thought-out the evening and had stuck to water and cola, giving the impression she was drinking vodka to her colleagues. She had been careful to be picked up on the hotel CCTV as staggering and unsteady when Drew and she had checked in. Now, she made sure that the self same cameras picked her up leaving the hotel. Making sure her face was turned away from the cameras, she ensured they captured, what appeared to be, Drew leaving the hotel room in the early hours.

She, of course, would claim to have been too drunk to remember anything when questioned about his movements. She would say she had passed out and could not confirm or deny anything. All that she could recall was that he was dressed when she woke, that had surprised her.

She walked out of the hotel, avoiding the doorman who was occupied with greeting another couple, looking for a bed in which to spend the rest of their night fornicating. They had just stepped from a cab so she jumped in the back. Lowering her voice she ordered the driver to take her to MI5's headquarters.

She had paid the cabbie with her head turned and out of his eye line. When he was questioned, he confirmed picking up man on the Strand at about three fifteen on the Strand and driving him to Thames House.

Entering Thames House had proved to be the easiest part. The night guard barely looked up as she swiped Drew's pass. She made a mental note to recommend a review of the security procedures as she entered the lift. She was beginning to get a crick in her neck from constantly titling her head from CCTV cameras.

She sat at Drew's work station and logged in on his terminal. The next phase was the key to the deception. She used her own ID and pass code to log into the system. She had put her pass code on her phone. Her phone was in her pocket. Now, if checked, it would appear that Drew had taken her ID and phone from her handbag, if the phone's movements were tracked during the course of the investigation. It would lead from the hotel to MI5s headquarters and back

With a couple of key strokes, she changed everything. She made no attempt to alter the encryption log that showed that Tim had made the crucial phone call in order to stand down the driver, which afforded the opportunity for the Russians to be killed. She just set up a trail showing that Drew had apparently accessed the log using her ID. When examined it would appear as if Denham had instructed him to fabricate the evidence against Tim.

She left and returned to the hotel, ensuring that CCTV captured it all. She returned to the room. Swapped clothes and dressed and made sure she woke Drew at six before leaving. The police, on checking the logs and video evidence, could only draw one conclusion and that was, Drew had used her to try and establish an alibi, using the fact that she was heavily intoxicated and in a drunken stupor to cover his tampering with the log to incriminate Tim.

"Now your turn, how come you have the phone? You gave it to Zhen Zhou," said Harriet.

Chapter 44

It was the eve of Harriet's birthday. She had just left the Flowering restaurant and waited outside. She watched through the window as Tim spoke with Zhen Zhou. The gaggle of MI5 agents continued to eat their meal as the two spoke.

"Tell me more about this Du Longwei," said Tim.

"What is there to tell? He has power. He acts for the Chinese here in the UK. They use him as a sort of 'Mr Fix All'. You want someone dead, he fixes it. You want someone bribed, he fixes it. You want money repaid, he fixes it," said Zhen.

"I don't understand. How can he weild power like that here, in the UK?"

"I cannot speak for all, Mr Burr, but I can tell you my tale if you are interested?"

"I am in no rush," encouraged Tim.

"Twenty years ago, this year, the British left Hong Kong and handed it back to mainland China. That, however, was the end of the process. The Red Chinese had been working on the return of Hong Kong for decades before the handover. Their agents, spies and enforcers had been steadily infiltrating all levels of Hong Kong society. Their weak area was the criminal gangs that ran the Colony."

"The Triad Societies?" interrupted Tim.

"Yes, the Triads," said Zhen. "The Red Chinese made attempts to take control the Triads, however they matched violence with violence, intimidation with intimidation and corruption with corruption, they could neither be infiltrated nor intimidated while the British were in control."

"And when the British left?" asked Tim.

"Those that did not kowtow to the Communists would be made to disappear."

"I assume you did not want to give in to them?"

"I was younger, just over thirty then and rasher, I planned to leave with my wife and six month old daughter and start a new life in the UK. I used my contacts and obtained passports and visas two weeks before the handover by the British to the Chinese we were set to leave. I was naïve. In my mind I saw my family and I, making a clean start, here. No more gang activity, I would as you say, turn over a new leaf."

"What happened?" said Tim.

"I got out, my wife and baby daughter, did not."

"They are still in Hong Kong?" said Tim.

"My wife is dead and my daughter is on the mainland."

"I see, and Du Longwei?"

"I am his lap dog, along with many others, who have family left in China. I must do has he commands, or my daughter will suffer."

Tim sat and thought about the situation. He had no liking for the drug dealer, extortionist thug sat across the table from him. He was, however, not the police. His job was clear. His priority was to defend the Country from the threat from terrorists and foreign powers. Not all threats came in the form of bombers and gunmen. The threat top of MI5 list, at the moment, was the Chinese attempt to hijack the steel industry and specifically, the new, light weight armour.

"I share a common gaol with you at this precise moment in time and that is the nullifying of the threat posed to the UK by Du Longwei. I need him gone from the game. If I help you with your daughter's predicament, I would expect reciprocity from you in return. Be very clear. I am not offering you any form of protection or immunity as regards your criminal activity. Personally, I consider you scum, the lowest of the low, a parasite. I will do everything in my power to assist the police in bringing you and your thugs to book. On the other hand, I can assure you that MI5 will not target you. We do not consider your organisation a security threat, merely criminals," said Tim.

"What are you offering?"

"Give me the name and location of your daughter. If I get her to the UK with a passport and a new identity, you will help me combat Du Longwei and the Chinese threat," said Tim.

"Get my daughter safe and I will wipe out every Red Chinese in the Country," said Zhen.

"That is not quite what I had in mind," said Tim. "I do appreciate the sentiment, but I should rather not start a war with China. Just dealing with Du Longwei will be sufficient. Now write down your daughter's details and give it to me."

Tim left the Flowering Lotus with the details in his pocket. He and Harriet then enjoyed a burger.

The next day Tim met Bernard Waverly, head of MI6 on the Embankment. He asked him to extract, Zhen's daughter, Ling Ling, from China. He then went on to the Coal Hole for Harriet's birthday drink.

Ling Ling returned to the UK as part of the trade delegation and was put up in the Monmouth Hotel, situated just a half a mile from China Town and the Flowering Lotus Restaurant, where her father, Zhen, ran his criminal activities.

Tim next found himself back in the Flowering Lotus, as the Chinese New Year's celebrations were taking place. The expert handed Gil's phone back to Zhen before he left.

"I am to phone Du Longwei now, I am to tell him that I have the phone and that it has been verified, that the plans are still on it," said Zhen.

"Which you will do," said Tim. He waited while Zhen made the call.

"Miss Shaw will be returned to you at the entrance to China Town, where the dancing is taking place," he said to Tim.

"May I have the phone?" said Tim.

Zhen gave Tim, Gil's phone. "My daughter?" said Zhen.

"At the Monmouth Hotel, ask for Sarah Spice. My men, protecting her, will release her to you, "said Tim.

"You have truly got her out for me. Thank you, thank you," Zhen had tears of joy at the thought of seeing his daughter, his daughter, a mere baby when he had fled Hong Kong.

"No problem, glad to be of service," said Tim. "I am off to get Miss Shaw back, now." He made his way out of the Restaurant.

Zhen turned to one of the young men. "When Mr Burr had his colleague in safe. Kill that piece of shit, Du Longwei," he said.

Chapter 45

"Well, how did the meeting go?" asked Harriet. It was a few days after the showdown at Thames House. Tim had just come back from a meeting with Moon, the Met Commissioner, the CPS and the Home secretary held at the Home Office.

"Well everyone is a lot calmer as the dust has settled. Moon apologised to me and the Home Secretary gave me a pat on the back."

"I think that was rightly deserved, after all, you single handely thwarted the acquisition of the Ban Dan Steel works in Port Talbot by the Chinese, recovered the plans that will allow Britain to become the World leaders in the new lightweight armour manufacture, disposed of a Chinese agent, provocateur and assassin, whilst exposing Denham's plot to doctor MI5's computer systems"

"All in a days work," laughed Tim.

"Seriously, what happened to Denham and Drew?"

"Well, there was little appetite to turn the matter into a scandal and have it dragged through the press. So pragmatism prevailed. I have to say that, as Denham and Drew were actually guilty of nothing, the outcome was the right one."

"So what was the outcome?"

"The usual, when someone is past their sell by date in the Civil Service, a knighthood and retirement for Denham"

"Sir Harry, perfect ring to it," said Harriet, "and Kevin"

"He is to be your personal assistant."

"What?" said Harriet?

"I knew how close you two became. I just knew you would relish being able to cuddle up on your lunch break and carry on your romance," said Tim.

"You are taking the piss?"

"Of course I am," said Tim.

"So what did happen?"

"He's fine. He is transferring to GCHQ with a clean record and a two grade up promotion. After all, he was guilty of nothing," said Tim.

"He was guilty as hell, "said Harriet.

"No, you set him up."

"Do you really think I would just set out to frame someone?" she asked.

"I am confused," said Tim.

"For crying out loud, how the hell do you think Denham got his hands on the evidence to give to Commissioner Moon to put you in the frame?"

Tim looked blankly back.

"Fucking Drew of course, I don't know what deal he did with Denham, but he, sure as eggs are eggs, did one. He accessed the security log and got Denham the stick to beat you over the head with."

"But how, he doesn't have the clearance?"

"He doesn't have the clearance, but he is top notch at programming. He hacked in and got what Denham needed. Fortunately for you, Tim, he is not as good as I am."

"How can he hack in, surely our system has to be one of the best protected?"

"It is, but all systems have weaknesses. The security service systems come under regular attacks from anything from school kids to foreign government. Most are dealt with in seconds, but just now and then a more serious attack occurs. Then we go into what we term lock down mode, in effect we pull up the drawbridge and stop all in and out traffic. It gives us the time to check things manually and deal with matters. There is an opportunity, when this happens, for the IT personnel to access files outside their security clearance to track and repair any damage that resulted from the attack."

"And Drew took such an opportunity to get Denham enough evidence to set me up?"

"In a nutshell, my esteemed leader, but sadly for our friend, he was not as smart as his boss. He did it, but not the night of my birthday. I just put the record straight. Why do you think he confessed? He knew that it made no difference now we were looking, eventually it would track back to him and so better not to take the risk. By confessing, he was certain to escape prosecution. If he didn't, there was the very real danger his real hack would turn up and he would end up in the clink."

"You can't trust anybody in this business, can you?" said Tim.

Printed in Great Britain
by Amazon